Chronometer

Camille Cabrera

Book Teaser:

One hour can change everything. For Evie Laythorne, those sixty minutes were the difference between life and death. She's the only person that really knows the truth about what happened at the top of the tower during that unexpected fall storm. If only walls could talk.

Dedication:

To my dearest nurse, confidant, trusted friend, and honorary grandmother. A woman with endless patience and a boundless vigor for life. Keep flying, Kathy.

A caution to the curious.

Monday

October 28th of 2019

Chapter 1

Fog rode into the harbor on the back of gray waves as they lazily lapped against the dock. Seals barked and battled over the floating slats of wood. Seagulls called to one another and plundered the communal trash bins for the perpetual supply of leftover fish and fries discarded by tourists.

It was a typical day in San Francisco, but then again, that statement was rather a contradiction. No day in the city of the Golden Gate Bridge was ever something as simple as ordinary.

Evie pulled her once plush floor-length jacket closer to her body to ward off the early morning chill. The wind took merciless bites from her hollow cheeks and left her fingernails a cadaver-like bluish purple. It felt like the elements were trying to devour her alive.

Her slim fingers reached into the deep pocket of her wool jacket and plucked out a red unopened pack of cigarettes. She then flipped open the lid and selected one at random. The fire from the lighter managed to partially illuminate her pale features and emphasized her large eyes that seemed too big for her angular face.

She welcomed the smoke into her lungs and held the drag for as long as possible. Eventually, she opened her red painted lips and casually watched the white tendrils of smoke as they languidly escaped her mouth and intermingled with the fog.

"Those things will kill you, Kid."

"That's the point."

Chapter 2

"That's not funny, Evie. I'm an old man and the normal order is that I beat you to the grave. Stop trying to make it a race," Jack Bloodborne scowled in disapproval at the slender woman who seemed determined to turn all of his hair completely gray.

"It's okay, Uncle Jack. I'm not trying to beat you. I just can't help being competitive. Did you get any new leads for me this week?" Evie absently ground the butt of her cigarette against the worn bottom of her shoe. The remaining embers withered away as several chunks of ashes fell onto the salty wooden pier.

Jack groaned. He knew Evie was too bullheaded to fully listen to his advice, but that never stopped him from trying. He cared for Evie like a daughter ever since he had taken her under his wing. Her parents had passed away about five years ago, which had placed Evie in a precarious situation where she was nearly too old for foster care, but definitely too young to enter a bar.

Jack had told Evie countless times to follow a different career path, but it only made sense that she ended up in a similar line of work. He held the highest ranking position within the homicide department in San Francisco. The job had taken a toll on his hair and turned it prematurely gray— a price that Jack seemed to take in stride, seeing as he considered it a badge of honor.

"You worry me, Kid. Why don't you look into other career paths? You're smart, and I'm sure you could pick something up like coding in no time. It's practically expected that all the kids your age are into computers around here."

"Silicon Valley doesn't embody the deeper soul of the city. It's for other hopeful people and not for me," Evie said, arching one of her dark eyebrows at Jack. It was a tiny show of defiance that wasn't pointed at Jack but more so against the industry that was slowly swallowing up San Francisco and spitting it out as a gentrified wasteland full of tech bros and finance Chads.

"You always had a soft spot for the salt of the Earth. It must be genetic. Your parents were wired the same way. They were always going on about the importance of personal virtue and fighting for the spirit of the city."

"Look where that got my parents. Sometimes I wonder if my mom would have been better off staying in Korea. Maybe she would still be here if she had picked another lover. Maybe her fate was locked into place from the start."

"Don't dwell on those thoughts, Kid. They only spiral down. Your parents loved and still love you. That's all that matters. You'll see them again when it's your time. Long after the worms have made a meal of me."

Jack folded his hands together as if closing the topic. He then looked around the desolated section of the pier and sighed.

The fog was slowly settling deeper into the city and each of its wintery talons were steadily wrapping deeper into the bay. Eventually, it would be so cold that even the bravest tourists would shy away from taking photos and exploring for the night.

"Let's get dinner, on me." Jack clapped his large paw against Evie's back.

He frowned as if he thought that he could knock her over with a little bit more force. Evie had a slender build for her height and Jack always joked that a brisk ocean wind would one day whirl her into the air like a discarded plastic bag. She'd swirl up into the clouds and float away with the wind until she eventually crashed back into the ground.

Evie found Jack's fatherly antics a bit dramatic but quickly relented at the promise of food. It wasn't like she was in a position to turn down a full meal. The private investigations barely covered her rent and rarely extended to power and utilities. It wasn't that people didn't need the service, Evie just hated the idea of charging people for her help. She often ended up investigating for days or weeks on end and then felt bad about delivering the news. It was always bad news, even when the client had thought that it was good. When people cried, and as their worlds imploded, Evie often found herself waving the fees. She knew deep down that she was too soft when it came to investigating, but it just felt wrong to kick someone with a price tag after finding out that their spouse was cheating or that the love of their life had an entirely separate family. It happened more often than not and Evie knew as soon as she looked into their pained eyes that she was a goner.

"Thanks, Uncle Jack. Where are we headed?"

Jack scoffed, "Don't act so green. We're getting Italian."

"Sounds good."

Chapter 3

"Can you pass the parmesan?"

"Thanks," Evie grabbed the shaker and poured a generous helping onto her massive portion of fettuccine Alfredo, the cheese dutifully piled on top of the already dairy-laden meal.

"That's an act of treason," Jack narrowed his eyes at the defiled pasta as Evie simply shrugged.

"Write me a ticket."

They ate in silence, and Evie looked around the partially full restaurant. It was a tight space with red leather booths pushed together. The chairs that often smacked into each other as patrons exited the center tables. Their lucky booth offered an unobstructed view of the street. People bustled outside. Some were heading home for the night while others were deciding which Italian restaurant smelled most alluring.

Evie took a few more bites and sipped from her fizzy cherry soda. The plastic straw poked into the roof of her mouth and Evie gave a sharp cough.

Jack took that as his sign to continue the topic from the pier. He casually set down one of the slices from his family-size pepperoni pizza and admitted, "I was hoping you'd be interested in taking on different cases. There are so many options that would be a better fit."

"What do you mean by a better fit?" Evie had an idea about what Jack wanted to say, but she needed to hear him say it out loud.

"You did an amazing job with that murder case. You put Danvers away and took a dangerous murderer off the streets. I could even put in a good word for you at whatever department strikes your interest. You have talent."

"Thank you, Uncle Jack. It was really the adventure that kept me interested, but I didn't really do much. Not in the end. Danvers killed himself last month."

"You're kidding." Jack's stoic face conveyed about the same amount of shock as his hollowed out words.

"You knew."

"I wanted to keep tabs on him."

"He supposedly hung himself."

"Consequences and actions. Not everyone has the stomach for both." Jack picked up his momentarily forgotten pepperoni pizza and took a large bite from the folded slice. He took another chomp from the crust while Evie mentally chewed over his statement.

His words didn't comfort Evie, but it was the thought that counted with Jack. He rarely managed to hit the mark when it came to emotional needs, but he always gave it his best try.

After a few minutes, Evie sighed, "That's part of the reason I don't want to work with heavier stuff. The jury was so quick to convict and there were still a few points that could have been stronger with more time. The evidence all pointed to him, but still."

"They were quick to convict because you made a solid case against the bastard. You'll come around once you decide on a path that's more fulfilling."

Once again, Evie decided to push. She nudged, "What do you mean by that?"

Jack groaned and wiped his mouth with two thin white paper napkins. He crumpled the paper in his meaty fist and said, "You need work that involves more than just dragging down cheaters and liars. It's dulling your spark. You have something special, and you're letting it burn out. I don't want that life for you. I don't care what makes you happy, but find it and do it. If you want to make balloon animals or breakdance by the pier, then by all means go for it. If your true calling is spelunking in abandoned homes for ghosts or becoming an artist who can barely afford to paint then do it. I just want you to be happy, and so does Madge. She worries about you like you're her only daughter."

Evie quipped, "Madge knows that I'm her only daughter. Your two boys are a handful and you need a little estrogen to help lighten the load."

"Exactly. We just don't want that light to burn out," Jack held Evie's gaze for a moment. He then nodded as if he approved of his attempt at a career intervention and no longer wanted to keep up the heartfelt conversation.

His words surprised Evie because Jack was a man of few verbal cues. Heck, when Evie had graduated from college, he had barely smiled. Jack had spent the majority of the celebratory lunch talking about the small plastic chairs and how the honorary speaker had taken too long.

Evie knew that Jack was proud and cared deeply but he simply had a funny way of showing it. He tried his best and that's all that Evie really cared about. Sometimes, Evie wished that he cared a little less.

Jack stuffed the last bit of crust into his mouth and washed it down with a generous swig of soda. Instead of trying to catch up, Evie took her time and finished half of her pasta dish. She'd save the rest for later.

Her index finger pressed around the tin container as she worked on the to-go box. Jack rested deeper into his side of the booth as the heaviness of the meal finally caught up to him.

Satisfied, Evie looked up and gave a small smile, "Thanks for the food, Uncle Jack."

"Anytime, Kid. Just don't get into any trouble."

"I can't promise that."

"I know." Jack patted Evie's shoulder and stood up from the booth. He gave a lazy stretch and waved at the hostess as he donned his dark walker coat.

He turned to Evie and called, "I almost forgot. Here are a few leads for your case with that slippery husband."

Evie frowned as she glanced at the outstretched thin manila envelope, "How did you know?"

"He's also wanted for fraud. It would be more convenient if his wife isn't in his good graces once that information comes into play."

"Always an angle."

Chapter 4

The Tenderloin looked rougher than usual as the sun disappeared behind a thin layer of stars. Shadows stretched out from the corners and greedily grasped at the city. Soon, the sun would set before five in the evening and then Evie would need to find her way home by streetlamp.

Street vendors were slowly packing up and heading home for the evening as shop owners locked their private places of business for the night and rolled down the metal door guards. Evie wasn't bothered by the graffiti along the rolling doors or the dirt caked onto the streets. She had grown used to the vibrant atmosphere of one of the most roughened but lively neighborhoods in the city. It allowed her a chance to breathe without the stuffiness and forced decorum that she often despised when speaking with clients in Nob Hill. There was too much pretense and too little substance. The entire situation made Evie's skin crawl, but she effortlessly pasted on an understanding and sympathetic glance when clients complained of increased prices on gluten-free bread and higher tuition at private schools for their kids. It felt like a completely different universe from the problems and annoyances in the

Tenderloin. It was hard to imagine that going just a handful of city blocks was similar to traveling to another planet.

Evie strode closer to her favorite newsstand and hurried across the street as a friendly figure reached for the door shutters.

"Joseph!"

The man stopped closing the shop and a friendly smile lit up his face once he noticed who had called his name so earnestly.

Evie hopped over a stream of undrained sewage water and debri. As she crossed the distance, she asked, "Slow day?"

Joseph shrugged his shoulders and handed Evie her usual newspaper. He replied, "Can't complain. Business is moving as usual and people still enjoy reading the papers. One day I'll have to close for good, but that doesn't look like it will be tomorrow."

Evie rolled her eyes and teased, "You're always convinced that you're going to close, but you've been on this corner for all four years that I've lived here."

"Twenty."

"What?"

"It's been twenty years on this street corner. I took it over from my father and I have no plans of leaving until the neighborhood kicks me out."

"They'll never want you out, Joseph."

The older man gave a proud smile that deepened the fine lines around the corners of his eyes. His brown skin was darkened from years in the sun and his midnight black hair was slowly getting flecks of gray. In some ways, Evie found Joseph to be a pillar of the community. Certainly, he was a witness to the rise and fall of a different era as Silicon Valley newbies came into the area and slowly tried to gentrify the city with toy poodles and almond milk. It was a slow cultural eradication that was as old as the tale of time.

Evie pulled out her money and traded Joseph for her prized paper as she ducked back under the half-closed metal gate and called, "Thanks, Joseph. I'll see you tomorrow."

"Sounds good. Buenas noches, Evie."

Chapter 5

Evie reached up and placed the third lock securely over her faded white apartment door. The smell of seasoned frijoles drifted into the room through one of the thin walls. The neighbors were cooking dinner, it smelled like meat and beans tonight. For a moment, Evie was tempted to knock on the door and ask to try some of the food that had always made her belly rumble in hunger. Luckily, when she glanced down, she realized that she was still holding her leftovers from the Italian restaurant in one hand and the newspaper in the other.

She walked the short distance to the kitchen counter and opened the pasta. A nerve in Evie's face twitched once she noticed how coagulated the cheese had become. The long walk through the city had cooled the food and made the cheese look somewhat plastic under the yellow glare of the overhead fluorescent lighting. The counters appeared more putrid than the advertised eggshell color that had been so boldly written on the for-lease advertisement several years ago. Even the fridge seemed a sickly shade of citrus thanks to the garish puke-colored tint that covered the room.

Evie quickly popped the leftovers into the microwave and sighed. Then she opened one of the cabinets and pulled out a clean glass. Her arms deftly reached up and plucked the bottle of whiskey from its hiding place inside the breadbox. She hadn't been sure if Uncle Jack would come up. His infrequent visits generally coincided with when he seemed most concerned about Evie.

The bottle was cool to the touch, a result of a barely functioning heating system from the 1950s. The heater wheezed and heaved near Evie's studio bed. A small grin graced her lips as she poured the brown liquid into a low glass right before the microwave chimed.

She brought her meal to a side table next to the plush armchair that overlooked the humming Tenderloin during the day. Evie put down her second dinner and carefully closed the curtains to avoid any prying eyes. In a city, the odds were that someone was always watching you whether out of simple curiosity or for some less innocent reason.

The fluffy chair felt wonderful against Evie's sore muscles. Her back ached from exhaustion as she tried to find a comfortable spot. She shoveled the reheated pasta into her mouth and sighed. The noodles were hot, but it wasn't the same as those first few bites in the restaurant. It tasted like a cheap reimagination from someone who wasn't exactly sure what a proper pasta dish was supposed to taste like.

Once the plate was devoid of even a single wayward noodle, Evie put it on the side table and turned her attention to the newspaper.

The grime from the ink and dirt smudged her fingers, but Evie didn't mind. In fact, she enjoyed the feeling of the gunk as she flipped through the thin evening paper and took her time reading the newest stories.

Apparently, some tourists had been arrested for disorderly conduct near Pier 39. The duo seemed to have barged into a famed chocolate factory and intentionally knocked over two pounds of hot fudge. The odd story caused a startled snort to escape from Evie's nose.

"Tourists," Evie muttered under her breath, taking a long sip of whiskey and welcoming the warm burn as it traveled to the back of her throat. The sensation moderated Evie's usually strained temper and grounded her as she read the rest of the evening news.

Tuesday

October 29th of 2019

Chapter 6

The bright morning sunshine cut through the clouds and pelted the concrete while street vendors enthusiastically called to the crowd. Evie winced as a luminous streak of light shined in her eyes. She quickly pulled out a pair of scratched sunglasses and placed them on her face. The lenses were covered in a thin layer of marks from years of sitting at the bottom of her massive, bucket-sized purse. Whether the imperfections came from being pressed against a pocket knife or a few pointy folders, Evie couldn't be bothered to tell. Luckily, they helped protect her from the unusually clear sunny day while she skulked around vendors and avoided loud groups of people as they huddled around shops and laughed with their friends.

Finally, Evie arrived at her intended destination. She walked into the newspaper stand and plucked her usual choice off the shelf. Out of curiosity, Evie looked at the other covers and noticed an image of a man clad in only boxers while obviously flexing his muscles while facing the sea. Another magazine cover featured a photograph of a gorgeous woman dressed in a ball gown, her body splayed over a magnificent horse.

The images were so over the top that Evie nearly laughed. Nearly. The two relaxed reads acted as perfect bookends that propped up the less than positive news stories.

Joseph claimed to intentionally separate the heavy newspapers on his shelves with lighter reads to avoid scaring off customers. He said that too much bad news or filth made a person unbalanced. Evie did not disagree with the sentiment, but she had a sneaking suspicion that Joseph simply hated organizing the shelves. She figured that the man, in his early seventies, likely didn't enjoy bending over to arrange the shelves due to his arthritic bones. Instead, he preferred to place items only once. One and done.

Evie grabbed the morning edition of her exceptionally structured newspaper and walked to the register. Small packets of candies and soda displays from the early 2000s littered the long counter.

"Morning."

The strange voice caught Evie's attention as she looked over the counter and noticed a slim man in his late 30s. His face held an exceptionally bored expression as he rang up the newspaper.

"Where's Joseph?" Evie handed over the change as her brows pulled together with worry. It wasn't like him to disappear from work. Heck, Evie remembered when Joseph had worked every day even when he had had a 102 degree fever. The man was as stubborn as a mule when it came to keeping the shop open.

The stranger gave a small shrug and handed Evie her change. After a minute, the man behind the counter said, "He decided to take a break and be with family."

The explanation didn't sit well with Evie and she couldn't exactly put her finger on why. She worried that age was finally catching up to her friend.

With a firm nod, Evie tucked the newspaper under her arm and headed out the door. She braced her body against the pesky sunlight as a mild headache pounded behind her eyes like a steady drum.

She decided that a change of pace might help her morning routine. Evie headed along the bustling streets and made a beeline for the closest trolley. She didn't want to bother paying for a cab when her feet and public transportation worked perfectly fine. Most days.

Eventually, Evie made it down to the water. The smell of salt surrounded her nose as seagulls cried out and protested against the meager amount of morning scraps. It was still too early for the larger lunch crowd that often left copious leftovers. The birds treated areas like the pier as their personal kitchen.

Evie walked over to an empty bench and settled into a comfortable position. There was a slow trickle of foot traffic for the early morning hour, and Evie knew it would turn into a steady stream of tourists closer to lunch. For now, she sat content in her own company. She took a sip of her freshly brewed coffee from one of the smaller shops along the pier and sighed. More than two hours after waking up, she was finally starting to feel more like a human. It was a task that had seemed almost impossible when Evie had first been jostled awake.

The newspaper pages stuck to Evie's fingers as she tried to flip to the next section. She wiggled her slender digits and then gave her hand a vigorous shake. The action pulled at a page and nearly tore it in half.

"Damn." Evie cursed under her breath and tried to hold the flimsy paper together so that she could finish reading the article.

Apparently, the mayor insisted on reforming the city by taking a stronger stand against homeless encampments. The removal strategies seemed to describe unhoused people as completely unworthy of compassion. Evie wrinkled her nose at one suggestion that claimed the city should wrangle the unhoused from the streets like cattle and then bus them out of the city to then drop them off near the mountains and deserts.

The suggestion seemed almost comical if Evie hadn't known just how serious the mayor was about eradicating the homeless by simply giving them the boot. It sounded like cheating to give up and toss out an entire group of people from the city.

The story vaguely reminded Evie of how she had been treated in the system after her parents had died and before Jack legally became her guardian. Thanks to legal limbo, she had spent about five months in the system, and it had been some of her roughest nights to date. She remembered how the other kids would pick on the newest house member every night. For four of those five months, Evie took the brunt of the abuse and simply tried to keep her head down. She had quickly learned that people often fed off reactions. The less she reacted when they tossed her doll into the toilet or cut her hair in the middle of the night with dull scissors, the less interested they were.

Evie knew that walking in the Tenderloin was like a carefree walk in the park compared to living in foster homes, where the system consistently turned a blind eye to what happened under certain roofs. It was easier and cleaner for the city and government to ignore the problem or to kick it out when the consequences didn't directly impact someone of financial or social value. However, as soon as someone fancy or connected felt inconvenienced, then the world shifted and twisted to accommodate and comfort them. The world gingerly coddled certain people and pretended others didn't even exist.

Evie closed her eyes as if the action could protect her from the nightmares called her past. At night, she tried to console herself by bringing memories of her parents to the surface. However, the darker times always seemed to find a way to slither into her consciousness. Deep down, Evie knew she would have turned out completely different if Jack hadn't found her and used every trick in his handbook and every connection under the sun to bring her home.

There seemed to be an endless supply of cruelty available to people that needed a helping hand. Evie found it hard to stomach. A morning drink seemed to call her name as she pondered over all of the unnecessary cruelty.

Displeased, Evie allowed the ripped page to crumple down as she flipped to the next story. The old article folded over and cowered as if personally ashamed of the content within its pages.

Suddenly, an image of the manicured greenery just outside of Coit Tower stood in the foreground of a photograph that did little to shed light on the larger story. The grass looked perfectly maintained and not a flower appeared out of place. The photograph of the area looked completely at odds with the provided information within the article.

Evie skimmed most of the paper as her eyes flitted from one column to the next. The stories were often continuations from previous news cycles, and many seemed sensationalized. Well, that and Evie knew the private details of many reported stories, and many stories were parallel, but still different from what was reported in the news. In news stories, the truth rarely overlapped in the right sequence.

Evie was just about to fold the newspaper and toss it into a bin when a headline caught her attention. She sat up straighter on the rough wooden bench. Her curiosity managed to get the better of her as she narrowed her eyes in concentration.

Evie repeated the story out loud, "Mystery woman is found dead on Telegraph Hill. Officials reluctantly ruled it a suicide. No sign of foul play and no leads on her identity. The woman is said to have fallen from Coit Tower during the early morning hours. No information on why or how the woman was able to enter the structure after hours."

The entire story had so many holes that Evie mentally envisioned a sinking ship. How could any person get into Coit Tower after hours without being detected? Why would someone go alone? Did she not have any identification on her at the time of her death?

Evie reread the story a second time to try and understand what had happened. A frown pressed between her eyebrows as she read over the story a third time. She ran her teeth over her lower lip and tried to understand why such an absurd story hadn't taken the front page for the day. How could a woman die so suspiciously on Telegraph Hill only to end up in the very back of the paper?

Her eyes desperately skimmed the story a fourth time as she tried to process what had caused the woman to die. Apparently, she had fallen from Coit Tower in the very early morning hours, and police had reluctantly ruled it as a suicide.

That information gave Evie pause. Why would the police rule it as a suicide if they weren't completely sure? Evie sat up straighter in her seat and anxiously licked her lower lip. What was going on here?

Questions whirled around in the back of Evie's mind as she wondered how that was possible. The article had captured her curiosity, and Evie instinctively knew that she wouldn't be able to let it go. She was like a dog with a bone when it came to interesting stories.

Evie pulled out a red pen from the inside of her jacket. It wasn't uncommon for her to have several odd items within her hidden pockets. For example, Evie had a lighter and two sticks of gum safely tucked away in the other pocket. She uncapped it with her teeth and held the cap in her mouth as she sloppily circled the entire story. The vibrant scarlet color wrapped around the bolded words and illusive picture in an angry red loop of ink.

She didn't understand the deeper meaning behind the words. They only hinted at the vaguest outline of the woman. It was like poorly describing color to a blind person.

The vibrancy of the spirit was missing and so was the depth required to fully paint the picture of a complicated and real person.

A shiver sped down Evie's spine as her eyes scanned the strange story for a final time. Evie sighed as the hairs on the back of her neck suddenly felt aggravated. She mumbled, "I think someone just walked over my grave."

She was too preoccupied with the story to notice the figure that lurked a few paces just out of sight.

Chapter 7

Evie unlocked her smartphone and scrolled to the calendar section. Her cracked screen made it difficult to decipher certain appointments. She used her thumb and index finger to enhance the image so that she would have an easier time reading the contents. Evie frowned and tilted the screen to the side so that it could better track her hand movements. Finally, after what felt like hours, the slow screen snapped into position, which allowed Evie to quickly read over her agenda for the rest of the week. It looked like she only had two current clients. Such an open schedule would allow her to have a fair amount of freedom. Which wasn't exactly a good thing given that she tended to spiral without clear parameters.

She took in a deep breath and decided to lock the screen. A sudden flash of pain pulled Evie's attention to her fingers.

"Damn." Evie looked down and noticed a sliver of glass, poking out of the top of her thumb. She had accidentally swiped too aggressively and as a result, a chunk of the chipped screen was now deeply lodged into her finger. It was her own fault. She had known for weeks and should have at least put some tape over that section in order to protect her hands. Unfortunately, other tasks always seemed to take priority. Live and learn.

Evie briskly walked over the uneven wooden boards as she decided to make a detour before delving into her two investigations. The curiosity was threatening to eat Evie alive. She promised herself that she would feed the ravenous hunger before it made a meal of her mental peace. Unfortunately, the bills needed to be paid and there was only one way to accomplish that goal. The hunger would need to wait.

Her quiet place near the water wasn't able to quell her anxious thoughts. She took in a deep gulp of air and plucked out another wayward chunk of glass from her finger that she had missed.

The seals barked and brawled with each other on the docks as if it was just any other normal day. Of course, to them it likely was a day like any other in the animal kingdom. The light energy that hovered above the water battled with Evie's own heavy emotions. An invisible cloud hung above Evie as she felt like the bringer of death and destroyer of worlds all before nine in the morning.

Unable to put off the inevitable, Evie walked over and decided to pay for a bus ride back into the heart of the city. One of the perks of having such particular clients from Nob Hill was their close proximity to the Tenderloin. The distance was no longer than ten minutes by bus, but it felt like a lifetime given the difference in lifestyles. The problems were different and so were the people, but Evie knew that at the core, most people desired to love and be loved. Which was why she had very little interest in earning her payment.

She eventually made it to the right bus stop and paid the rather large fee. The distance between Nob Hill and Pier 39 was too long of a trek for so early in the morning.

Evie sat down at the back of the bus and breathed in the exhaust fumes as they crept through the open windows. She watched as parents with their kids and preoccupied office workers hopped on and off the bus at various stops. Some unhoused members of the community also used the buses for transportation given that it was more affordable.

The bus was idling in traffic and the fumes were starting to make Evie sick. She tried to distract her mind by looking outside the smudged window. Homes and shops passed in a blur as people walked around the city with a sense of rushed self-importance. Everyone was in a hurry to go someplace and be someone while Evie was just there, feeling stuck.

The ride wasn't long enough. In less time than Evie cared to admit, she ended up outside of a luxurious cheery yellow townhouse. The street held a certain charm as small trees were placed in allotted spots along the sidewalk and luxury cars remained parked at an angle along the gently sloped street. The hilly sidewalk offered a generous view of the bay. Quiet townhomes presided over the lower areas of San Francisco with an air of old money superiority.

Many people from several generations back, often claimed that Nob Hill was the Upper East Side of the city. Evie wasn't inclined to disagree with that assessment as a nanny crossed the street with a Pomeranian carefully tucked into an enclosed baby stroller. The small purse pooch dutifully barked at every falling leaf and pigeon along the way. Alongside the nanny, walked a child of about four years old. The toddler remained tethered in close proximity to its carer by a dog-shaped backpack that was attached to a leash.

The irony of the situation momentarily stopped Evie from walking up the last remaining steps to the canary colored townhouse. Once the trio grew a little farther away, Evie placed her attention back on her current task.

She gripped the manila envelope in her hand more tightly and struggled to compose her features. Her client had given her a hefty sum to prove that her husband was cheating. Unfortunately, the information that Evie had found stretched a little deeper.

Evie raised her hand and pressed the doorbell button attached to the camera. The white cylindrical box beeped and a posh disembodied voice promptly called, "Coming. Thank you for your patience."

A few minutes passed before a slight commotion occurred on the other side of the door. Several chains and locks moved across the wooden surface until the door finally opened to reveal a woman in her mid-forties. Her pale skin was marked by sunspots from many days likely spent out on the water with a sailboat. She wore pale brown chinos and a neutral colored top. Her hair was slicked back into a low bun which gave the impression that she had either just rolled out of bed or hosted a tedious conference call.

Given the time of day, Evie was tempted to believe that the woman had just woken up, but combined with the knowledge of Mrs. Haversham's business ties that option seemed unlikely. Mrs. Haversham chose to work from home, but maintained a considerable amount of influence when it came to the technology sector.

"Come in." Mrs. Haversham politely entreated and brought Evie back into the moment.

"Thank you."

Mrs. Haversham flawlessly guided them into an elaborate sitting room that looked much larger than what Evie had anticipated from the outside. A plush white sofa sat near a large bay window and let bright morning light into the room. The windows were so vast that it momentarily reminded Evie of living in a fish bowl. It was likely that the majority of the formal living room was visible to the street.

"Can I interest you in a cup of coffee or a glass of water?" Mrs. Haversham anxiously asked Evie as she sat in a tall wingback leather chair.

"No, thank you."

"It's probably best. I gave the help the day off so that we can speak freely. You will be at my mercy when it comes to the kitchen. A small price for privacy." Mrs. Haversham gave a small forced smile as she tried to keep the mood light.

"That's a smart choice." Evie kept her back straight and gripped the folder that was still in her hand with a force much stronger than necessary. Her fingers were tense as if the folder was liable to make a run for it at any moment.

Evie reached out her hand and gave Mrs. Haversham the lightly filled envelope. Unsurprisingly, she accepted the envelope with the same amount of eagerness that a person would have when agreeing to touch a venomous snake.

The woman's face instantly paled as she read over the information that she had so desperately begged to obtain.

Over the years, Evie had learned that the best approach when delivering difficult information tended to be a direct and respectful one. She tried to put the information out and into the open without making the process take any longer than necessary. Evie tried to be a merciful executioner for already floundering marriages.

Slowly, Mrs. Haversham opened the envelope and pulled out all of the contents. A shaky pale hand covered her mouth as her eyes grew glassy with tears.

Evie respectfully averted her eyes to the plush thick white rug. The expensive material looked completely untouched as if the entire room was often unused.

A small sob caused Evie to pry her attention away from the richness of the fabric. Evie's eyes remained impassive as Mrs. Haversham's mouth kept opening and closing like a fish gasping for air. She was likely searching for the right words in order to ask her final question.

Eventually, Mrs. Haversham flipped around the photo. It showed a man in his mid-fifties with a woman about ten years younger. They held hands and smiled as two small children followed behind in their wake. The kids looked like exact photocopies of the adults.

A shaky finger pointed at the young girl with two ponytails and the small boy without his two front teeth. Mrs. Haversham demanded that Evie finish what she had started.

"Who are they?"

"They are your husband's children. He has another family in Pacific Heights."

Tears trickled down Mrs. Haversham's face and left smudges in her once perfectly applied makeup. Her lips were permanently drawn downward as spots of water and mascara dampened the collar of her shirt.

Evie kept her eyes glued to the imposed photograph as she replied, "He has been with the woman for at least five years. The neighbors know him and believe that he is a traveling real estate investor."

Mrs. Haversham's lips pulled back into a wounded snarl as she barked, "He wouldn't know how to invest in real estate if the exam book hit him over the head. The only thing that Mike knows how to do is take. I made a life for us. I gave him an allowance and several credit cards because he doesn't work. I never made mention of his disinterest in work after the accident. He claimed that getting a job would be too stressful on his heart after his last heart attack. Like an idiot, I agreed. That was fifteen years ago. After so many years, I have finally worked hard enough to give us this amazing life. I gave him everything he ever wanted, but he never really gave me what I wanted. What I needed. Well, what I always needed to become."

Evie finally looked up at Mrs. Haversham. The once perfectly composed woman looked so much smaller than when Evie had first walked into the house. A slim hand cupped her flat belly before Mrs. Haversham's fingers traced the image of the two children in an almost reverent fashion. Now, Evie's client looked unmistakably small as the large chair threatened to swallow her whole.

The nosy curiosity that Evie so often wrestled to the back of her mind managed to break free. In a moment of weakness, Evie asked, "What?"

Mrs. Haversham sank further into her seat as her glassy blue eyes pierced deep into Evie's soul. She whispered out, "He said that he was infertile."

Evie wasn't sure what to say. Her mouth opened and then closed. It was as if she had forgotten how to speak. Some moments weren't right for words. Instead, Evie reached out and held Mrs. Haversham's hand in a comforting grasp.

The contact was light, but obvious enough to offer support.

Mrs. Haversham's eyes were clouded with pain as she weakly returned the contact and implored, "Let's get a drink."

Normally, Evie found tasteful ways to back out of the requests. Unfortunately, something about Mrs. Haversham pulled at her heartstrings. She sucked in her lower lip and shrugged, "I could use a drink."

"Perfect, let's call a car. We can use my husband's only personal credit card. No promises on how much we will be able to drink. It has a low limit."

Mrs. Haversham stood to her feet with an unknown strength. She quickly rearranged her makeup and hair into a perfectly timeless and sophisticated bun. Evie followed quietly behind as they headed out the door of the visually picture perfect home.

A few minutes later, lights from the Fourth Sentinel illuminated the sky. Two doormen rushed to open the glass paneled doors as Mrs. Haverhsam floated in. Evie followed behind like a phantom or more accurately like a small child hiding behind the legs of a parent. Evie's jeans and ratty hoodie had nothing in common with the opulent chandeliers and intricately designed carpet. Evie noticed a grand piano in the lobby as a sophisticated and obviously accomplished pianist played a smooth jazz melody.

Onlookers barely gave the pianist a second glance. It was almost as if he were there in the same capacity as music on the radio or a game on the television. Not that such a sophisticated and renowned place would ever think to use such items to add to its ambiance.

Mrs. Haversham walked directly up to a man behind the counter. As soon as the man noticed Mrs. Haversham, he stood up straight and gave her a small respectful bow as he said, "Mrs. Haversham, it is so lovely to see you again. The usual table?"

"Absolutely, bring another bottle this time. I have company."

"Of course." The man turned to Evie and to his credit, the smile behind his eyes only momentarily faltered. He had looked at Evie and seen exactly who she was. In the blink of an eye, he understood that she likely frequented the tourist shops of the Fisherman's Wharf in search of a fancy meal instead of a five star hotel for a few drinks. It wasn't her world, but neither of them made a single comment.

His nametag gleamed with the role of manager and it seemed rightly earned. Understanding people before they ever said a word seemed to be one of the most priceless gifts that a person could ever hope to have, especially in this city. It was one of the reasons why certain people managed to get promotions and why others couldn't seem to catch a break. Like the saying goes, read a room.

Currently, Evie wished that she was illiterate. Every corner of the room practically read displeased with her presence. The table closest to them had a woman that had pulled her purse closer to her chest as if Evie intended to snatch it from the back of the chair and sprint from the hotel.

Evie refused to give any sort of indication that she had noticed the gesture and instead chose to look straight ahead. The promise of a drink and an expensive free one at that, was enough to tempt her into swallowing her pride. Besides, the last thing that Uncle Jack needed was a call about how his favorite niece had lost her mind and murdered half of the towns snobby elite while trying to get paid by one of the wealthiest women in San Francisco. Evie wasn't sure what would upset Jack more, the idea of Evie finally snapping and killing someone or the knowledge that she continued to pursue a career that slowly murdered her from the inside.

A waiter in a freshly pressed white shirt approached the table and did a gesture several inches lower than a bow to Mrs. Haversham. It bordered on a genuflect. Evie watched the interaction similar to how a child analyzes a bug. She felt like yelling at the waiter as he kept his gaze fully focussed on Mrs. Haversham. Childishly, Evie glanced at the waiter and imagined picking apart his invisible wings. For some reason, the man reminded Evie of a grasshopper with his hoppy steps and long legs. Unsure if a deranged smile was showing on her face, Evie grabbed the menu and held it above her mouth.

She kept watching the interaction and wondered if wildlife experts experienced a similar feeling. Evie felt an odd mixture of curiosity and distress at the interaction. She desperately wanted a glass wall to separate her from the opposite side of the table.

"It is so wonderful to see you again, Mrs. Haversham. Will you be having your usual?"

A sound crackled in the back of Mrs. Haversham's throat. It seemed similar to the grinding of glass shards as she laughed, "No. Today we are in the mood to splurge. Please bring us your most expensive bottle of wine to start."

The waiter's eyebrows nearly disappeared into his hairline as he asked, "Would you like to know the region and the year? Perhaps you would like to taste it first?"

The shock within the man's voice told Evie that this bottle likely cost closer to what she made in an entire year. Clearly, he had no intention of dissatisfying a heavily paying customer by ignoring her wishes or bringing her a lackluster bottle of wine.

Mrs. Haversham waved away the concern and added, "Not necessary. Just make sure that the price of the bottle is enough to make a person flinch. Please get something to drink, Evie."

The menu was still pressed so close to Evie's face that she couldn't decipher the words on the page. Instead of taking a moment to look, Evie answered, "A cup of coffee, please."

"That's all?" The sudden ice in Mrs. Haversham's tone instantly made Evie backtrack on her financially paltry order.

Evie nervously licked her lower lip as she added, "Vodka on the rocks."

Mrs. Haversham raised an unimpressed eyebrow, but her previously ruffled feathers settled into a more relaxed pose as she instructed the waiter, "Top shelf and bring the bottle."

"Of course, Mrs. Haversham. The waiter vigorously nodded his head and then sped away.

Mrs. Haversham leisurely turned in her seat with an ease that surprised Evie. Every second, Mrs. Haversham grew more confident and shed her veneer of meekness. The transformation momentarily shocked Evie, but she took it all in stride. Suddenly, Mrs. Haverhsam's eyes darted to Evie's face. For a moment, the imposing blue gaze seemed similar to the world's largest telescope, but just as quickly the moment of inspection ended.

"I loved him so much that I went blind." The words left Mrs. Haversham's lips in a similar fashion to how people discuss the weather.

"How did you go blind?" The deeper meaning behind the words enticed Evie's curiosity. Additionally, asking questions ensured that Evie wouldn't need to answer any inquiries about her own life. The strategy wasn't purely selfish, but it did offer Evie some security from prying eyes. It was always easier to refrain from sharing personal details with clients.

Mrs. Haversham placed her chin into her cupped palm and sighed. The years that she had now deemed wasted appeared much more obvious as they manifested into tight lines between her eyebrows. It was as if the unpleasant times had carved a pathway around her skin like a shovel against gravel. The skin around her lips dented inwards, likely from stretching one too many times into an emotionless smile. Mrs. Haversham seemed to be a contradiction of newfound vigor and sudden exhaustion.

"I didn't want to marry him at first. In fact, I didn't even want to speak to him again after the first time that we had met. My gut had told me no from the very first time that we had spoken. It was like a tiny little voice in the back of my head had screamed at me not to see him, but I had pushed it down."

The waiter arrived with a gold encrusted bottle of wine and a tall slim bottle of vodka. He gingerly placed the bottles on the table and announced, "This is a cabernet sauvignon from the year 2012."

Mrs. Haversham waved the waiter away before he could finish his explanation. Undeterred, the waiter simply nodded his head and poured a glass of wine for Mrs. Haversham before he retreated to a different corner of the ornate dining room.

Perspiration glistened on the bottle of chilled vodka and Evie casually nodded in approval at the ostentatious label that she had always admired on bar menus, but never touched.

Mrs. Haversham noticed the appreciative glance and Evie quickly disguised her knowledge with an intentional bungle. Evie tapped a finger against one of the spotless wine glasses and said, "They didn't give us ice."

Mrs. Haversham's curiosity about Evie instantly disappeared. The intentionally clueless remark hit its intended target and drew all suspicion away from Evie. Within less than one second, Mrs. Haversham had easily accepted that Evie came from a lower standing. Obviously, the physical appearance of Evie's worn jeans and tattered shoes further bolstered the sentiments.

"The wine is chilled, Evie. We just need to let it breathe. Let's start with the vodka while we wait." Mrs. Haversham made two overly generous pours of the clear liquid and then handed a glass to Evie.

"Thank you. What were you saying earlier about that little voice?"

Mrs. Haversham nodded her head and quickly downed about a third of the clear content in one go. She didn't even flinch as she returned to the previously abandoned story. She ran a single finger down the side of her glass as her mind traveled back to past events that only she could see. Mrs. Haversham continued, "I ignored that little voice in an aspect of my life where it mattered the most. Somehow, I stupidly tried to come up with convoluted reasons to give him a chance. Do you know the number one reason that I came up with?"

Evie looked at Mrs. Haversham's pinched face and replied, "Manners?"

"Exactly. My reason for seeing him again was because it was polite. I had fought against the little voice in my head because for some reason I couldn't stand the idea of inconveniencing him and looking impolite. I was afraid to look rude. Well, damn manners to hell. Listening to that little voice could have saved me millions of dollars and years of my life."

"People see what they want to see. Even when it never existed."

Mrs. Haversham groaned, "How are you so intelligent?"

Evie took a measured sip of vodka before she answered, "I'm not. My job teaches me about people and patterns. After a few years, it's pretty easy to read and understand people. It's harder to read and understand yourself. The real trouble comes when you get the two confused."

"What I wouldn't give for a career change. That seems like an extremely beneficial job." Mrs. Haversham tossed back the glass in one fluid motion.

"Seems like it." Evie parrotted the words, but they tasted bitter against her tongue.

Mrs. Haversham carelessly poured two glasses of wine and some of the liquid sloshed over the rim of the glass and trickled down the crystal stem.

Instinctively, Evie reached out and swiped away at the drop. It stopped mere centimeters from the pristine tablecloth that looked as fresh as new snow with a thread count that was easily double that of Evie's own bedsheets.

"You didn't need to save the tablecloth. This town can use a little bit more red. Besides, my lovely husband can just pay to have it replaced. This entire afternoon will all be courtesy of his personal credit card. He always uses mine so now it's time for him to return the favor." Mrs. Haversham tossed back another drink as her tear-filled eyes burned with fury.

Evie tried to soothe, "That's fair. We can ring up the charges for him."

Apparently, the answer had surprised Mrs. Haversham as wide blue eyes stared at Evie in shock. The older woman asked, "You're not going to give me an entire speech about how wrong that is? Isn't that your job, to keep people accountable?"

Evie sighed as she took a slow sip of vodka. The warmth traveled down the back of her throat and offered her a sense of comfort. Eventually, she answered, "This job was supposed to be easy and clear-cut. Expose the bad people and get paid. Simple. Black and White. But the longer I'm here, the more I see that most people have a little gray in them. People aren't just one thing and that's what makes this job so hard. How do you hold the line when it's invisible? Sometimes it's more about making the best call one step at a time." The alcohol had managed to loosen Evie's tongue.

Mrs. Haversham squinted at Evie's face, "You could have just said that you hate your job."

Momentarily stricken, Evie wasn't sure about what she had expected as a reply, but it certainly wasn't such a frighteningly honest response.

Mrs. Haversham slurred her words as a dark look overtook her usually cheerful features. She anxiously glanced around the room and ensured that no one was looking. Luckily, the table was placed a distance away from the others in one of the more isolated sections of the restaurant.

Satisfied, Mrs. Haversham pulled her purse off the back of her chair and placed it into the center of her lap. With great care, she cautiously unzipped it. She angled the opening of the purse so that the contents were just visible behind the pristine tablecloth. A glimmer of silver metal stole Evie's breath away.

Chapter 8

Mrs. Haversham's gaze looked crazed as she proudly held the unzipped bag and tilted it at an angle so that Evie could easily view the deadly content.

"A life for a life. He stole so much from me." Mrs. Haversham caressed the side of the gun with her long spindly fingers.

Without hesitation, Evie swatted away Mrs. Haversham's fingers and plucked the firearm out of the Italian leather purse. Evie tucked the gun into the back of her pants in one swift motion. Her fingers ghosted over the safety and ensured that it was still in place. A relieved sigh passed her parted lips. Evie kept her gaze hard as she looked at Mrs. Haversham. It was a similar look to that of a frustrated mother scolding a petulant child.

Neither woman said a single word, but they spoke volumes with their eyes. Eventually, Mrs. Haversham blinked and the moment was over, but not forgotten.

Evie picked up one of the remaining menus on the table and asked, "Do you think that he can buy us some food?"

Mrs. Haversham grabbed the other menu, "Absolutely, let's make it hurt."

"I can get behind that." Evie shifted in her seat and the cold metal of the gun left frigid butterfly kisses against her lower spine.

"Do you like meat?"

"Love."

"Perfect. Get two dishes and don't forget to leave room for dessert."

Evie simply nodded her head as her eyes took in the menu for the first time. The promise of death long forgotten, Evie frowned at the insane prices. She rarely spent that much money on essential items like rent and now that same amount of cash was about to pay for a delicious, but unreasonably expensive chunk of cow. Unwilling to rock the already unsteady boat, Evie decided on one of the generous steaks and then explored the seafood options. Evie considered it a rare occasion whenever her fish wasn't covered in fried batter.

In due time, the bill arrived and even Mrs. Haversham visibly flinched at the amount. A satisfied grin crept along her lips. She resembled a cat that caught the canary as her perfectly manicured nails tapped against the edge of the bill. Mrs. Haversham signed and even included a three-figure tip for the eager waiter. A gesture that Evie had been made aware of as the waiter had sprinted out of the dining area, convinced that there had been a mistake. After several reassuring words, the waiter had enthusiastically waved goodbye to Mrs. Haversham.

The early evening chill invaded Evie's body and managed to heighten her previously dulled senses. An odd prickle of awareness slithered down her spine and made her falter in her steps. Evie's gaze sluggishly searched around the area as her mind and gut remained slow due to a remarkable combination of high-end meat and alcohol.

"Evie, the car is here." Mrs. Haversham's impatient voice pulled Evie away from her search. If Evie had scanned her surroundings a moment longer, she would have noticed the man tucked behind a few sparse bushes. The light from the end of his cigarette flickered in the wind before it was unceremoniously snuffed by the breeze.

Chapter 9

The fabric of Evie's coat felt like it was on fire. Her hand grew warmer with every passing second as her fingers remained curled around the edges of Mrs. Haversham's hefty check. Evie bit her lower lip as she imagined the generous check that was stuffed deep within the confines of her outer pocket slowly burning a hole into her hand. Evie flexed her palm and involuntarily crinkled the paper.

Her chest felt heavy as she struggled to take in a fresh gulp of air. It was as if a weight was pushing into Evie's lungs and making it impossible to breathe. After thinking it over, she decided that it would have been more humane to simply shoot Mrs. Haversham between the eyes. Put the woman out of her misery. Better yet, Evie should have put Mr. Haversham out of his misery and allowed Mrs. Haversham to sort out the details. After drinks, Evie had practically sprinted out of the once cheery townhouse as if the hounds of hell were on her heels.

Disgust weighed heavily within Evie's belly as she walked at a brisk pace down the sidewalk. She needed to get as far away from the blasted canary colored home as possible.

It wasn't because Evie was simply upset by both of the Havershams. No, Evie was absolutely repulsed by her own actions. She refused to look at her reflection as she passed several massive pristinely clean apartment windows and storefronts. It was just her luck that all of the windows on the street seemed to have been recently washed.

Evie wanted to disappear from the city. However, she knew nothing else and the idea of leaving felt impossible. Evie felt inexplicably tethered to the streets and to her mundane life. She was stuck without the slightest idea as to why. Evie had been glued to the streets and skyline all the way to her bones. It was as if her life had been jammed into neutral and she couldn't figure out how to get the gears to change. In some odd way, the routine and consistency gave her a strong sense of comfort, but she also desperately resented it. She hated that her job consisted mostly of breaking people's hearts. Worse, most of the time the people already knew, but refused to give up hope without substantial proof. Hope was the worst part. She had recognized it behind Mrs. Haversham's eyes. Evie's semi-honest words had snuffed it from Mrs. Haversham's hopeful gaze like a harsh wind against a singular candle.

In Mrs. Haversham's case it was both beneficial to the larger San Francisco police force and to Evie that her husband was so blatantly crooked. Now, Mrs. Haversham would likely demand a divorce and drain her con artist partner of the funds that he so desperately needed to woo and entrap other women.

Evie hadn't been completely honest with Mrs. Haversham. The family in Pacific Heights wasn't the only family unit where Mike liked to play house. Evie had followed him around for two weeks and had found two other women and another family unit with small kids. The exact details didn't seem necessary in driving home the point to Mrs. Haversham. Besides, Evie reasoned that Mrs. Haversham could easily hire more private detectives or do additional digging if she felt so inclined. Apparently, Evie didn't have the heart to twist the knife for the final strike.

Her feet aimlessly walked the streets and Evie decided to let her mind wander for a few hours. She felt adrift and unreasonably restless in a way that had quickly become familiar in the recent months.

The emotion had first reared its ugly head only a few days after the solved murder case. Evie remembered how proud she had been. For the first time, Evie felt like she had a larger purpose. She had a sense of pride in her work.

The simple cases quickly faded in vibrancy and interest. She had realized over the past few months that there was very little reason for her cases. A marital dispute or a scorned lover. Of course, there was the occasional concerned parent or lost family member and those cases always held a special piece of Evie's heart, but those requests were often few and far between.

After about an hour, Evie realized that she had ended up walking in an extremely large loop. Her thighs burned from trudging the steep streets without paying attention to the inclines or cracks in the cement. She had stumbled several times as her feet dragged against the ground. Like a mindless machine, she had continued the meaningless pattern. Finally, Evie looked down and sighed at the new scuff marks on her shoes which only added to the visible disrepair. These were her nice shoes.

Her thoughts had managed to get the better of her. It appeared that there was only one option left that could possibly provide her with a sense of meaning.

Evie decided that she needed to solve the mysterious murder on Telegraph Hill. The story in the newspaper had been calling her name for days. She wondered if solving it would give her a sense of peace.

Of course, any sense of true purpose would be a welcome change from delivering heartbreaking news to people that already suspected the worst case scenario. On the odd occasion that Evie was sent to find a lost relative, it brightened her day. The point was closure and that was something Evie deeply understood and often craved.

Murders were a grizzly business for the obvious reasons. What people often forgot about death was that loved ones were always left to pick up the pieces. A person's story never ended with their own death. A version of the departed lived on with each person that had known them in life. Some versions tended to be much more glamorous and flattering than others. Devastating loss often brought out both the worst and best versions of the people left behind. It released the raw emotions carefully hidden behind well-practiced veneers.

You would think after countless lifetimes stretched out over millions of years, the human species would have learned to cope with death. Instead, it seemed that death managed to catch no one and everyone by surprise, every single time.

The point of an investigation into a murder was often just as much to provide justice to the living. To help comfort the people viciously robbed of their loved ones. There was a practical aspect to catching a murderer. A righteousness in preventing more precious life from being snuffed out before its time. Then there was also a more intangible, but just as important part of a case where the loved ones of the murdered were finally able to get closure. Closure in a sense that the fog of unanswered questions had finally cleared from the shores and given people the ability to understand what had happened. It would never give life back that had already been lost. The knowledge would never replace the person. However, it could help give the people left behind the opportunity to live and heal. It was the worst consolation prize on the planet, but it was something.

Decided, Evie sighed and looked up into the bright sun as a chilly breeze blew through her straight dark locks. Evie hoped that she was making the right choice by branching out into a new case that wasn't even hers to begin with.

Wednesday

October 30th of 2019

Chapter 10

The broad brim of the black baseball cap covered the majority of Evie's face in shadow. She slumped her shoulders lower than usual and donned a forced air of disinterest. With her body posture one step away from invisible, Evie easily entered the area of the Financial District where she knew that her next assignment was located.

Evie understood that her mark wasn't aware of what she looked like, let alone that she existed, but that didn't stop her from being cautious. She had no interest in scaring away her assignment and losing out on being able to pay her rent. Besides, she usually ended up waiving the fees when the person that hired her started to cry. It was a tireless circle and Evie struggled to stay between the lines.

People in suits strode around the streets. A few held cups of freshly brewed coffee while others walked with their heads down, completely invested in their phones. Evie was grateful that so many people were physically present in the area. Especially, when a generous amount of them were too distracted to remain focused on the present moment. It made Evie's job so much easier when people weren't fully paying attention. She walked down the street and kept a carefully practiced air of insignificance wrapped loosely around her slouched form. Her hands were shoved deep into the worn coat pockets of her best jacket. Each step was slow and measured as she turned the corner and looked up at a tall silver high-rise building. The windows seemed to comprise the majority of the exterior as it proudly stood in the heart of the district. The building remained steadfast as it reached up into the sky and defied the heavens. Each window was spotless. Commotion caused Evie to look up. She turned and realized that a crew of cleaners were making their way down the side of the building using a moving platform. From her position, she couldn't even see the slightest indication of bird droppings or dust, but somehow that didn't stop the workers from cleaning at a nearly superhuman pace.

The process momentarily mesmerized Evie as she stopped near the opposite side of the sidewalk and watched as the members of the team made quick work of a large section of glass. Their movements were methodical to the point that Evie wondered if robots would ever be able to achieve such precision. There was something oddly beautiful about how each person on the platform knew their job as well as the job of their partner. To achieve such unity, each person needed to know how every member of the group functioned.

Evie squinted as she tried to understand if such an awareness was inherent or constantly communicated throughout the duration of the task. The cleaners were so high in the air that she doubted that she'd be able to hear anything that they said. Her eyes locked on their faces, but she couldn't see any mouths moving.

In the time that Evie stood near a half-wilted planter, the group had managed to finish a chunk of the building spanning two levels. Evie nodded her head and allowed herself a moment to marvel at such a job.

Personally, Evie despised heights. She rarely ventured out onto balconies and almost never went to a rooftop bar even though they were completely guarded and designed to prevent accidental falls. She hadn't even been on a flight in over five years. Evie had claimed that it was an issue of finances the only time that Jack had asked, but in reality the thought of leaving the ground only jostled Evie's nerves. Her aversion to heights had only increased after the death of her parents. Evie never wondered if there was a correlation, but she figured that it was possible.

She tilted her head back and noticed that the roof of the building had a metallic pole sticking out from the top. It gleamed with a vibrant red light that warned evening pilots about the sheer height of the building. It was a structure that stood several stories too tall for Evie's liking, but she needed the money. Hopefully, she wouldn't need to use the elevator. Maybe she would get lucky for once.

Evie stretched out her sweaty palms within the confines of her tattered jacket and braced her body against the impending wave of panic. She glanced into the lobby as a sharp sigh escaped her lips.

Several people on the street looked in her direction and Evie quickly covered the blunt reaction with a cough. It appeared that she wouldn't need to get into an elevator to reach the top floor after all.

Mr. Blackthorne had contacted Evie to find proof of his wife's infidelity. It was a task that Evie didn't relish, but she was unusually good at executing. Mr. Blackthorne's wife stood in the lobby of the busy building with a small grin on her face. Her figure and face were an exact match to the woman in the photograph that Evie had received from an unknown phone number. The similarity was uncanny. Evie had a sneaking suspicion that Mr. Blackthorne had sent her a photo taken during the previous weekend. He had told Evie that he had spent a restful weekend with his wife in Yosemite. Apparently, the trip wasn't enough to convince him that his wife was simply tired of his monotone voice. Evie knew that wasn't fair. Most people seemed to know when their spouse was cheating without needing irrefutable proof. It was something that seemed almost like a detective's hunch or a gut feeling. The small details that added up to an unignorable amount of doubt.

Mr. Blackthorne's wife stood less than an inch away from a handsome young man that had a devilishly playful look plastered across his face. The look hinted at something less than strictly professional. Of course, it was possible that what Evie had interpreted as more than an innocent glance was simply her own mind projecting. Evie always struggled to keep a hold of her own imagination because it was very possible to see and connect fake clues when searching in the wrong direction. The younger man looked closer to being the woman's son with a gap in age that likely spanned between ten and twenty years. Given his behavior, he appeared to be a secretary of some sort as he playfully handed Evie's target a cup of steaming hot coffee and a bright red sticky note.

The woman in her mid-fifties read the sticky note and her cheeks instantly turned a dark shade of red. Her features were square and her jawline was broad, but her wavy brown shoulder length hair softened her traditionally tough features.

Evie muttered under her breath, "Come on. Give me something that I can use."

She couldn't take a photo of the woman holding a sticky note and claim that it had been a raunchy note without any substantial proof. Either she needed to get the note in question and document the content in person or she needed photographic evidence that showed an intimate relationship.

Evie nibbled her lower lip and grumbled in frustration. How was she going to get a photo of the duo when it was obvious that they were trying to keep the nature of their relationship a secret?

The pair stood close together and the man that was likely around Evie's age bent down and whispered something into the shell of the woman's ear. He leaned over and gently caressed the back of Mrs. Blackthorne's neck in a more intimate than necessary gesture.

Evie unintentionally lowered her gaze and gave the two a moment of privacy. She felt conflicting emotions bubble to the surface of her consciousness as she looked at the scene. The duo seemed so completely happy as they stood in the lobby and chatted. They were unaware of the task that Evie had been sent to execute. She had been instructed in no uncertain terms to find proof of a reason to end a marriage. Proof Evie now felt confident that she would easily get.

In all honesty, Evie wasn't sure how she felt about marriage after watching so many failed and explosive relationships. The jaded feeling had easily tainted her opinion of the union. From a legal perspective, the concept of a marriage made sense, but from an emotional perspective marriage seemed to make even the most levelheaded person vulnerable. The thought of willingly opening up to another person made Evie's skin crawl. She was much happier alone.

Evie's lips unconsciously pulled down into a small frown as the young man in a smart black suit offered his hand to Mr. Blackthorne's wife.

"Don't do it. At least, wait until I leave."

Evie chanted under her breath as she looked at the two people that were completely unaware of the other individuals in their surroundings.

The duo walked away from the center of the lobby and headed over to the rarely frequented restrooms. They built a brisk pace and Evie fought the urge to roll her eyes.

"Fine. Get caught." The words were barely out of her mouth as she jumped into action.

Evie followed behind a man in an expensive business suit and slipped into the lobby.

She kept her steps measured and light as she turned behind the elaborate elevator waiting area and followed at a generous distance behind Mrs. Blackthorne.

No longer visible to the entire lobby, the pair reached out and held hands. Evie quickly pulled out her phone and accessed her camera. She made sure that the flash was off before she snapped several quick photos. She quickly dipped into a small alcove that sheltered a barely-visible service door from view. From the hidden position, Evie took a video as Mrs. Blackthorne leaned up and kissed the man that wasn't her husband.

Evie kept recording from her hidden position only several feet away from the unsuspecting couple. Her lips pressed into a thin line as she kept her gaze on the phone screen. The images of the intimate moment captured on the phone provided a much needed barrier between Evie and the reality of the situation. It didn't feel as real when she looked at life from behind a screen.

Evie tapped and pinched the smartphone screen as she widened the shot. The wider image ensured that future viewers such as Mr. Blackthorne would have a better understanding of the setting. Evie made sure to get the restroom sign in the background and captured several different angles of Mrs. Blackthrone's face.

At that moment, Evie felt nothing. She felt numb as her finger robotically clicked away. Eventually, the couple grew more frenzied and disappeared into the bathroom.

Heels clicked along the lonely hallway as a dark haired office worker walked down the tiled area. She was about to enter the bathrooms, but she then looked down at her phone and spun back in the opposite direction. Close call.

Evie watched the near catastrophe from her secret spot near the center of the hallway. She tentatively took one step out into the open. Evie inched away from her hiding space and then quickly sped back to the safety of the lobby. She slowed her pace and mindfully matched the other individuals as they navigated the building at a casual speed. The average pace didn't exactly indicate an eagerness for work. People seemed to falter and procrastinate before taking the elevators.

Evie slid out the front door behind a frazzled delivery man and took in a large gulp of air. She tried to calm her nerves as her fingers furiously clenched her phone. Evie's palm turned white from the pressure. She couldn't look at the images just yet. Instead, Evie walked down the street until she noticed a small fast food joint.

The smell of hot dogs and warm grease wafted out onto the street and called to Evie like a siren song. She walked over to the counter and greeted, "Hi. One hot dog and a large black coffee."

"Sure. Coming up. That'll be $7 flat." The stout man wiped his hand over his sweaty brows and then rang up Evie's mismatched breakfast and lunch request.

Evie stepped to the side and sat at a table for two in the corner of the cramped restaurant. A group of construction workers sat closer to the front and laughed together as one of their buddies accidentally dropped a glob of mustard onto his shirt. Their levity in any other situation would have lifted Evie's mood. Unfortunately, she found that her spirit was practically tethered to the ground.

She unlocked her phone screen as her finger hovered over the saved images. After a few seconds, Evie gathered her courage and looked at the photos. She selected a random picture of Mrs. Blackthorne.

Evie licked her lower lip and winced at the obvious intimacy that was portrayed within the photo. Mrs. Blackthorne was angled extremely close to her male counterpart as her fingers gripped his hair. The man's eyes glittered with a sort of passion that Evie had only seen in films. He looked deeply into Mrs. Blackthorne's gaze.

Mrs. Blackthorne looked back with an intensity that matched his.

The next photo looked just as damning. Frustrated, Evie swiped her index finger against her phone screen and once again saw one of the videos that she had so quickly decided to shoot. The couple looked practically starved as they devoured each other in public.

There was no doubt about the cheating. Mrs. Blackthorne's face had been clearly visible from several different angles and the video evidence helped to portray a more realistic context to the scene that photographs so often lacked. The videos added enthusiasm that surely made any sort of explanation or excuse impossible to create.

"Hot dog and coffee!" A deep baritone voice shouted from across the shoebox-sized restaurant.

Evie stood from her seat and mumbled, "Thanks."

She walked back over and hunkered down into the metal seat that vaguely reminded her of an electric chair with its firm back and imposing weight. She no longer felt like digging in.

The hot dog looked charred and the bun was stiff, but it was warm and smelled delicious. Unfortunately, Evie no longer had the stomach for such a heavy meal. Her slim fingers picked at the stale bread. Her gaze followed the people that scampered by the massive panes of glass.

Evie took a bite and forced the mystery meat into her nearly empty belly. She reached out and gripped the paper coffee cup in her hand and sighed. The coffee would be fine in a few hours. Ashamed of how little she ate, Evie folded the paper plate in half so that it hid the barely touched hot dog. She tossed it into the plastic trash can near the door and then headed back out to the street. Not for the first time, Evie wished that she could disappear into the crowd.

Chapter 11

The wharf looked mostly abandoned from Evie's corner of the damp wooden platform. She puckered her lips around a cigarette and drew the smoke deep into her lungs. Evie held it there for a moment and allowed the nicotine to work its way through her body. Her eyes were fixated on something in the distance that she couldn't really see. It was a shape across the bay that managed to elude her sight at such a shadowy time of day. The shadows played with each other and made it impossible to really know what was on the other side.

The cigarette was half-finished and Evie winced as the ashes crumbled to the floor. She hoped that they wouldn't ruin her best pair of walking shoes.

In such a hilly city, it was nearly impossible to wear heels or unsupportive shoes without running the risk of muscle spasms or blisters. Evie didn't exactly enjoy heels and preferred to stick to more comfortable footwear. She liked options that tended to be more resistant to the city's grime and darkened puddles.

Her order of fish and chips had cooled from its once near-boiling temperature. Small amounts of steam still rose from the fish, but it was nothing compared to before.

A small meow caught Evie's attention as she glanced down and noticed a scrawny alley cat. The feline looked extremely malnourished. Its spine seemed to stick out from underneath a thick dark coat that emphasized its bright amethyst colored eyes.

The thin creature rubbed against Evie's legs and gave a deep throaty purr. Its dark tail wrapped around Evie's lower calf almost like how a petulant child would hold the hand of its mother during a particularly long grocery store trip.

Another indignant meow ricocheted off the wooden floorboards and Evie carefully stepped over the persistent tiny pest.

"I hear you. No need to shout."

The little cat followed obediently behind as its long tail twitched in irritation. Its purple eyes narrowed in what Evie imagined was an expression of impatience.

Evie placed the nearly finished cigarette between her slightly chapped lips as she used both hands to pull apart a particularly large chunk of fish. She ripped away the battered layer and hoped that the oil-soaked fish would be okay for the furry demon that vigorously yowled only a few inches away from her toes.

"You really are persistent. I'm going to give you a bite in a minute. I'm not sure if you're allowed to have greasy foods, but since I'm sure you like to dumpster dive, the oil on this fish is probably the least of your problems."

Evie caught herself talking out loud to the cat and sighed. After a momentary pause, Evie muttered under her breath, "I really need to get out more. I'm starting to hold conversations with strays."

Evie glanced at the cat as she bent down and held out a hand with a somewhat less greasy amount of chicken. She kept her hand still as the cat tentatively sniffed the air. Small whiskers twitched against the side of Evie's palm before the cat hesitantly withdrew as if unsure of the offering.

The smell of the cigarette remained strong in the air and temporarily stuck to Evie's fingers. It was a powerful scent that seemed to seep into Evie's pores. It didn't matter how much Evie washed her hands, the scent still managed to linger for hours. It was a constant reminder for Evie to get her next fix.

Dismayed but undeterred, Evie tossed the fish a few inches away. The stray cat jumped back, but then sniffed closer to the meat. After a few moments, the feline gobbled down the offering and made a small growling noise as it devoured the bargain meat.

In seconds, the fish had disappeared and the cat licked at the wood for the faintest traces of the treat. Evie walked over to her meal as it rested in a red and white checkered paper tray. It looked hardly edible at best, but her new companion didn't seem to care.

Evie cleaned another portion of fish from the oiled batter and separated the chunk in half. She decided that one more ample slice would do.

"Here. Take this, too. Don't get any ideas. I'm rarely reliable so you're going to need to keep getting your real meals on your own. I bet this area is crawling with fat rats."

Evie squatted down and hovered with most of her weight placed on her heels. She kept her hand extended and waited for the cat to approach.

Slowly, the feline crept closer with its ears pushed down onto its head. It sniffed the air once again, but this time crept a little closer. Tentatively, it grabbed the piece from Evie's fingers and hunched over the find as if a pesky seagull would swoop down and steal it at any minute. It seemed like a possible scenario given the amount of birds that often stole meals from tourists. Luckily, the impending promise of darkness had dulled the insistent commotion as the squawking seagulls settled in for the night.

Absently, Evie stroked the fur of the abyss colored cat. She felt its spine as her fingers gingerly traveled the scrawny length of its lean body.

"You'll be okay, Titan. You just need to get comfortable on your own, but not too comfortable. I'll probably bring you dinner from time to time."

Evie scratched behind one dark furry ear as the cat that she'd randomly named Titan licked its front paws. The meal seemed a distant memory as the little ball of fur cleaned the remaining oil and grime from its paws.

The moment of peace was ruined as a sharp burning pain emanated from Evie's lip.

"Damn!" Evie cursed as she dropped the now burnt butt of the cigarette onto the ground. She had forgotten that it had been carefully tucked into the corner of her mouth.

The embers faintly glowed in the dying strands of sunlight. Titan glanced down at the cigarette with a look of disdain.

"Judge away. It was a stupid move." She gave the cat a small frown and stood to her full height. The waves crashed against the rocks below in a slow consistent manner.

Evie glanced down and vigorously stomped out the remaining spark.

Chapter 12

Water splashed against Evie's shoe as she tripped over the dilapidated curb and accidentally landed in a deep puddle.

"Damn."

Evie glanced down and kept her foot submerged beneath the murky water for a second more than necessary. She narrowed her eyes at the filth and then gingerly shook out her soaked foot.

Her shoe squelched against the concrete as she walked the final blocks back to her home. An exhausted sigh escaped her lips as she glanced around the now mostly abandoned street. The shops had already closed for the night and only a few people roamed around in the distance.

The two and three-story buildings seemed almost crooked in the flickering light from a dull streetlamp. A few bugs buzzed near the glare. Evie was too busy trying to adjust her shoe to notice the figure that loomed just ahead in the shadow of an alley.

Evie shoved her nearly frozen fingers deeper into the freezing confines of her thin jacket. She tried to get a grasp on her phone. Evie had forgotten to call Jack earlier in the day and she didn't want him to worry.

Suddenly, a rough hand reached out and pulled her into the darkness of the alley. In less than a second, Evie disappeared from view.

Chapter 13

Evie gasped as she dropped her phone. Her hands roughly reached up so that she could wrap her palms around the broad arms of her attacker.

The stench of street urine and garbage entered her nostrils as a large palm easily warded off her hands and firmly covered her mouth. Evie's jaw ached at the pressure as the man behind her tightened his grip.

During moments of crisis, people tend to respond in unpredictable ways. Evie instantly thought back to all of those impromptu self-defense lessons that she had attended with Jack. She recalled how Uncle Jack had always playfully spared with his sons after dinner when they were all growing up. He had constantly insisted on escape routes and deflection to avoid being stuck when confronted with a tough attacker. Jack also encouraged fighting dirty when it came to dire situations. He claimed that anyone that wanted to take a life didn't deserve the mercy of a fair fight.

Fair enough, Uncle Jack.

The sudden flashback played in Evie's mind as clear as day. Jack had told both of his boys and even Evie that the most important part of any physical fight was using your brain. He had stressed that muscle was important, but would usually lose to a person with a calm mind and a clear plan. That tip was convenient given that Evie had little in the way of muscle on her slim figure. Most days, she was made of a single meal of fish batter and vodka.

Evie rolled her eyes at the memory as she dug her nails deeper into the stranger's wrist and bit down against the skin of his palm. She chomped and clenched her jaw to the point that she tasted the tangy coppery flavor of blood against her tongue. The stranger behind her grunted in protest. He desperately tried to retract his chubby hand. Evie allowed the stranger to retreat as she took several large steps away and established some distance between their bodies. She spit out the stranger's blood, but a streak of it dribbled down her chin and fell onto the dark alley floor. Evie's vibrant gaze glowed against the low light. Her features were relaxed and harshly juxtaposed the furiosity behind her stare. Blood freely trickled onto the hem of her blouse. It was as if every drop of blood was cleansing a space for a much darker ritual than robbery.

Evie narrowed her eyes as she glared at her attacker. She realized that the man was likely in his mid-forties. His pale wrinkled skin looked leathery from years of exposure to the sun. The grime on his clothes spoke of a hard life, but his hair appeared freshly washed and combed. The observation was brief, but critical as Evie instinctively tried to commit every detail to her memory. She guessed that the man was about five feet and ten inches tall and somewhere between 190 to 200 pounds. He was definitely in a different weight class than her if it came down to exchanging blows.

"Hands in the air, Lady." His accent held a soft southern twang that grated against the cool night air. His dark eyes looked like two bottomless pits threatening to consume Evie like an endless black hole.

Slowly, Evie looked at the man and noticed the long knife clutched in his left hand as it faintly glimmered in the sparse alley lights. The blade was several inches long and resembled something similar to what a butcher would use to sever a particularly stubborn cut of meat.

Evie's gaze turned blank as her eyes tracked the man's every move. At that moment, they were the only two people on the planet. Two people stuck in a wasteland of empty crates and broken bottles. She carefully weighed her next move. Her back faced the entrance to the alley and Evie wondered if she would be able to spin around and sprint out to the main street. She figured that such an attempt would likely turn out unsuccessful. The chance of getting a large knife into the back felt all too possible.

Instead, Evie watched a droplet of sweat as it trickled down the side of the man's face. His hand wavered slightly and Evie was willing to bet that the instability wasn't from adrenaline. The faint lines of track marks that crawled up the man's left arm helped to confirm her suspicion.

"Give me your wallet, Lady. You might be able to live if you don't get any funny ideas." The man's hand shook as he extended the knife and pointed it at Evie's chest.

Carefully, Evie reached into her outer pocket and pulled out a slim card case. Its shape was permanently stretched from a countless number of credit cards. Evie held it above her head and kept her eyes leveled with the stranger. Her eyes were blank and her face donned a neutral mask as she tossed the small card case several feet away. The tiny wallet fell deeper into the alley with a light thud as it clanged against the side of a large trash bin.

Evie never once looked away from the man as he kept the knife raised and pointed in her direction. She took in a measured gulp of air. Evie wiggled her toes and tried to stay alert. She had no reason to plant her feet into the ground when her best option was to flee. The movements came to Evie like second nature. Her entire body felt like it was on autopilot as she went through the motions without even batting an eye. She kept her stance light. Evie just needed to wait for the perfect moment to sprint away.

The knife lowered a few inches as the stranger took a step deeper into the alley. He then took another step closer to the general direction of the discarded wallet. However, his dark eyes made a cursory glance over Evie's frame and the look made a shiver travel down her spine that had nothing to do with the chilly night air.

A sickly dark grin crept along Evie's lips as she kept her hands up in a non-threatening position. Her curved mouth threw her assailant off-balance.

His brows pulled together in a combination of confusion and unease. He grunted out, "What's so funny, Lady? You think that this is a joke?"

Evie tried to suck in her lower lip. She hopelessly failed at wrangling in her emotions as she said, "It's pretty funny if you think about it. Out of everyone in the entire city, you found the one person that's been waiting for this excuse for years."

Her blunt confession momentarily threw the man off-guard. In his confusion, the stranger took a large step back as the knife slipped from his hand and clattered into a wayward puddle. His brows pulled so tightly together that they almost appeared to be touching.

"What does that mean, Lady?"

"It means that most people are looking for a good reason to die and I've been trying to find a good reason to live. You're going to need to try a little harder to scare me. You can't scare me with something that I've wanted for years. This would be the perfect excuse."

The man recoiled several feet as if Evie had physically slapped him. He stuttered, "Don't think like that, Lady. There has to be some reason that you want to be here."

"What's yours?" Evie tossed out the question so casually that it took a moment before the man was able to fully process it.

"Mine?" The stranger parrotted the question two volumes higher than his previous pitch. His eyes looked two sizes larger than normal and it reminded Evie of the spooked barn owl that she had seen in the trees near the Transamerica Redwood Park as a kid. Permanently startled.

The silence spoke volumes. Instead of saying another word, the man quickly turned on his heels and fled deeper into the darkness of the alley.

Evie waited several minutes as she stared into the dark abyss. Her eyes weren't able to decipher the stranger's outline, but her ears heard him as he stumbled over uneven concrete and rummaged around near the discarded piles of trash that were already placed outside for early morning collection.

Satisfied, Evie walked backwards and kept her face aimed at the darkness. It spiraled and swirled with each step as if the darkness was a sentient being just waiting for a chance to strike and pull her down. She took several tentative steps backwards until the light from the sidewalk finally greeted her highly alert senses. The glare from the sparse street lamps now felt overwhelming. The occasional light from the shuttered shops was now blinding. Evie walked deeper into the glow and stood in the middle of the street.

A passing car furiously honked at Evie as it drove around her dazed form. The driver rolled down the window and gave Evie the bird. Evie didn't bother reacting to the motion. She remained impassive as her mind raced to take stock of the altercation in the alley.

Her fingers dug inside of the secondary layer of the large bunchy coat. Frigid fingers ghosted over the outline of a much larger wallet. The bulky outline of the object helped to center Evie. She stepped onto the sidewalk and headed in the direction of her apartment. This time, Evie stood a generous distance away from the mouths of the allies. She had little interest in getting swallowed whole a second time.

The wallet that she had tossed to the stranger was a fake. He was going to be sorely surprised once he realized that the wallet was filled with expired credit cards and a grand total of $6. Evie had collected a few credit cards from random mail offers. For a whopping $3, Evie had bought a small black pleather card holder that surprisingly managed to get her out of a sticky situation. For less than $10, Evie had foolishly tempted fate and won. She was lucky that the thief had been too rattled to confront her about the lack of funds.

As a private investigator and a woman living alone, Evie was a big fan of contingency plans. Finally, after several years of walking around with a fake wallet, the day had finally arrived where she needed to use it. Not that she had much to protect. She had about one old reading chair to her name. A small smirk crept along Evie's lips.

She didn't really care about the wallet anymore. The thrill of the moment was slowly fading away. Evie was impressed with how her entire body had reacted from an odd combination of instinct and practice. Years of listening to Jack talk about how to handle an assailant had somewhat flown out the window at the first sign of reality.

Worse, Evie had practically goaded the man into ending it all. The action had managed to frazzle her attacker to the point that he had scampered away into the darkness of the alley like a scared stray cat. It had been a 50/50 bet.

A few older teens walked down the street as they headed out for the night. The kids donned corny costumes so that they vaguely resembled superheroes and vampires with a minimal amount of effort. One of them simply taped a long blanket to the shoulders of his black t-shirt so that it looked like a cape. The bright white beach blanket was a creative touch as it blew around in the air while the kid impersonated a flying superhero. His friends laughed and clapped him on the back as they headed on their way. The raucous laughter bounced off the buildings and filled the street long after the group was out of sight.

The joyful scene felt so out of touch with what had just happened to Evie. In the span of less than five minutes, Evie had managed to escape an alley with her life just to witness teens experience the electric joy of tasting their first few wisps of freedom. She always found it odd that people could have the worst day of their life just inches away from someone that had just received the best news imaginable. Evie knew that the world kept spinning even after people died. She had witnessed that firsthand with the passing of her parents. The world intertwined and then separated people at random. However, as a detective, Evie resented the idea that anything was random. She refused to believe in the idea of a happy coincidence or a stroke of random luck. There was a reason for everything and sometimes those explanations weren't packaged in bubble wrap or tied with a bow.

Evie kicked a loose stone. She watched as it skid across the ground before eventually tumbling into the street.

Thursday

October 31st of 2019

Chapter 14

Sweat poured down Evie's pale face as she gasped for air. Her fingers gripped the thin sheets so roughly that her knuckles turned white. She frantically looked around her apartment, but her eyes searched without finding. Eventually, her sight adjusted to the darkness and she could decipher the outlines of her chair and lamp as she sat upward in the small creaky bed.

She glanced over at the sparse nightstand and noticed an opened bottle of wine. It looked empty. A white mug had a bright red circle near the bottom and told Evie that she hadn't left a drop to spare. Evie had sworn that she had only drank a glass or two, but the evidence didn't lie. The entire bottle of a cheap merlot remained proudly situated on the dilapidated table. Mercifully, Evie couldn't feel even the slightest signs of an impending headache. She usually had the worst hangover after even a single glass of cheap wine. The sulfates bothered her head and often made it an almost impossible task to leave the apartment before noon. It was a miracle that she could sit up. Evie ran a hand through her disheveled hair and tried to tame at least some of her long dark locks.

"Damn."

Satisfied that a bad dream likely inspired by the cheap wine had caused her to wake up, Evie sank back onto her elbows and surveyed her surroundings. Light from the neon sign across the street crept along the corners of the room and landed directly on her old reading chair.

The clock on the nightstand held bold red digits, indicating it was just before four in the morning. A groan left Evie's lips once she realized that it was too early to leave the house and start the day, but it was also unlikely that she would be able to fall back to sleep. Again, she was stuck. Stupid dream.

Evie's mind tried to grasp at the remaining wisps of her possible nightmare. Unfortunately, the task proved unsuccessful. It was like reaching out and trying to get a grip on fog. The shroud of tepid darkness slipped through your fingers until it eventually receded and completely evaded capture.

The newspaper from three days ago sat discarded on the seat of the worn reading chair. Evie narrowed her eyes at the pages of stale reading material.

"What are you doing there?"

Unsurprisingly, her question remained unanswered. She thought that she had tossed the paper into the trash bin. Uninterested, Evie looked away and retreated back into her mind. Snippets of the forgotten dream moved behind Evie's closed eyelids as she recalled the faintest hint of what it had all meant.

In the dream, Evie invisibly followed behind the woman that had died near Coit Tower. Evie had walked each step up the winding staircase as her gaze had remained solely focussed on the dark outline of the spectral figure. It was too dark for Evie to see the stranger's face, but she felt like she was seeing a ghost.

The sensation had lasted throughout the entire dream and Evie had jerked awake just as the woman had leapt to her death. The feeling of falling had jolted Evie back into reality. Evie couldn't recall how exactly she had ended up at Coit Tower. She didn't understand why her dream had felt so disturbing. A sense of finality rang in Evie's ears. She often had dreams about past crimes that she had solved, but never about a current case. The dreams always followed her as if replaying the past on a loop. It was the first time that the dreams had decided to skip to the present, or was it the future? Worse, the woman from Coit Tower wasn't even an assigned case. Evie had simply read about it and now she felt obsessed. Haunted.

Evie rolled to the opposite side of the bed and placed her feet onto the worn wooden floorboards. She winced as the extreme cold seeped into her toes. The building was too old to offer central heating so most mornings the floor felt like an icebox. She blindly padded along the ground until her heels landed on her slippers. The back of the slippers were ripped and the fuzzy lining was mostly torn off, but it still did the job.

The sound of shuffling added to the empty room and only further emphasized the unpleasant silence. One of the reasons that Evie enjoyed the neighborhood came directly from its vibrancy and noise. She didn't exactly consider herself part of the community, but she still liked hearing the joy and sensing the levity from an outside perspective. Evie walked the neighborhood in a similar fashion to how a lonely dog warily circled a home that fed it scraps.

Evie shuffled into her kitchen and opened the top cabinet. She pulled out a bag of ground coffee and loaded a few scoops into the coffee maker. Another glance at the clock on the microwave told her that it was just a few minutes after four in the morning. There was no way that she was leaving before the sun decided to shine.

After last night, Evie wasn't afraid, but she was warry. In an odd way, the entire experience had left her invigorated. For the first time in months, Evie had actually felt alive. She usually went through the motions and accomplished goals for work, but very few of her tasks left her feeling something.

Anything.

In fact, most of what Evie did caused her to shut down and want to crawl deeper into her own head. Anything to hide from her own dismay.

The coffee pot created a constant drip as Evie stood watch over her treasure of dark liquid sludge. Her mind wandered back to the woman from Coit Tower. She wondered if there were some details that she had missed the first time that she had read the story in the newspaper. It was worth a try.

The last few drops of coffee trickled into the bottom of the pot. It looked like tar as it filled just above the maximum capacity line. Steam whirled up into the air and Evie took in a deep inhale of the hazelnut scented brew.

Delicious.

Evie poured a generous cup and breathed deeply as the calming scent worked its way into her lungs. She sighed as the warm mug thawed her nearly frozen fingers. The terror from her dream still lurked around in the back of her mind. It bothered her in a way that she struggled to put into words.

Her eyes once again trailed over the paper that she had so ardently sworn had been thrown away. Evie didn't believe in signs from the universe, but this one felt like an extreme exception.

She padded over to the worn leather chair and flicked on the switch of the old floor lamp. The lamp had been in the apartment when Evie had first moved in. It looked like something out of a noir film and fit perfectly next to the worn chair. The two items made a fool's throne room that was fit for a downtrodden private detective.

Evie hunkered down into her chair and leafed through the pages. It wasn't long before she landed on the story that had managed to take up most of her free time. The image of a featureless figure floating up the stairs of Coit Tower stirred in the back of Evie's mind.

She read over the story and took her time with every sentence. Evie didn't want to miss a single detail. The entire story seemed so tight-lipped. There wasn't a single mention of a witness or of a person that had found the body. Heck, there wasn't even a sympathetic quote from a police officer.

"Odd," Evie mumbled the word under her breath as she took a gulp of the freshly brewed coffee. The heat scorched her tongue and caused her to gag. So much for tasting breakfast.

Speaking of breakfast, Evie wondered if it was light enough outside to start the day. She had spent a fair amount of time reexamining the article and had let her mind wander to almost every possible alternative. She had decided that it was extremely likely that the woman had stumbled upon something unsavory and became a person of interest to a powerful individual in the city. If so, it only made sense that they would have kept journalists away and scrubbed her memory from the tabloids. With the right amount of money, the sky was the limit in a massive city. It wasn't exactly a solid theory, but it was the best that Evie had.

A quick glance out of the smudged windows told Evie that she could start getting dressed. The smallest sliver of light crept along the horizon and announced the start of a new day.

Evie glanced down into the street as the initial morning commotion began slightly earlier than normal. She noted the street vendors and shops proudly displaying calaveras in all different sizes and colors. Día de los Muertos was just around the corner.

In her own way, Evie revered the dead. She found that the past souls often brought families and friends from different generations together.

Even the distractions of life weren't enough to fully escape the exploration of death. It was the second act. The next journey. The final grand destination. After investigating so many grizzly cases with Jack, Evie called it a typical Thursday at work.

Evie glanced over at her bread box and wondered how much whiskey she had left. Her supply was likely running low. She made a mental note to stop at the small liquor store on the corner before heading home.

"Damn, the kids." Evie turned her attention to the streets below and saw several children dressed in Halloween costumes as they shuffled off with their parents before school. She also needed to grab candy to put outside for the avid trick-or-treaters.

The clock on the nightstand read that it was almost six in the morning. It was time to leave the apartment and receive some well-deserved answers.

In less than ten minutes, Evie tossed on a clean long sleeve shirt. She pulled on a pair of flared jeans, shoved her toes into her worn shoes and winced. A desperate squelch escaped from the shoes as water pressed out from the soles.

Evie grabbed the shoes and roughly tried to shake out the sneakers. It was a sorry attempt at air drying. She was about to place them on the newspaper, but hesitated. Instead, she grabbed two paper towels and plopped them on the window ledge. The nearly ruined shoes sat on the towels and Evie hoped that they would be able to dry out before she needed them. It was a longshot given that the entire studio apartment rarely went over 65 degrees during the fall. There was a fat chance of drying them out, but she still decided to give it a try. Evie had no interest in getting blisters while researching a murder that she already had no

business investigating. What Jack didn't know,
wouldn't hurt him.

Chapter 15

Evie's footsteps pounded down the stairs as she headed out on her mission with a renewed sense of purpose. First, she needed the newest edition of her morning paper. It was her daily ritual and although Evie wasn't particularly superstitious, she was extremely predictable when it came to her set routine. There was no reason to change it now.

Her daily activities felt almost ingrained into her muscles. It was as if her body already knew where to go without her mind needing to take charge. Each step followed the other without so much as a hitch. The only slight difference from usual was that Evie kept a generous distance away from the mouth of the alleyways. Although at this time of day, it likely didn't matter as the crowds of people flowed consistently near the edge of the alleys. The stream of people partly trickled into the shadowed areas that hid discarded trash bins and barred windows.

Mindful of the curb, Evie leapt from the center of the slim street to the sidewalk. She dodged around a small girl that tossed her hands up into the air and ran along the pathway giggling with glee. Her dark shiny braids rushed around her face as her fairy costume reflected the morning light. A flustered woman with equally inky hair ran only a few steps behind as she shouted a warning in Spanish.

A bemused smile itched along the corner of Evie's lips at the sight. The fairy wings on the costume bounced up and down and made it look as if the innocent child was practically gliding down the street. Shop owners retracted their brooms as they cleaned the street outside of their businesses. Vendors pulled their more expensive items out of the tiny butterfly's joyful and uncoordinated path.

Eventually, Evie turned her gaze to Joseph's newsstand. The blue awning looked as new as ever as it gently moved back and forth in the breeze. The store was old, but extremely well-loved. Joseph's deep pride in ownership of the quaint corner shop was clear.

Evie entered the store and looked over at the counter. The same man from earlier in the week had his face tilted down as he texted on his phone. His brown headphones bobbed up and down as he slowly kept time to a beat that Evie couldn't hear.

Disinterested, Evie silently walked away from the counter and headed over to her usual spot. The cover of today's newspaper held a sight that Evie would have never expected in a million years. She opened and closed her mouth like a fish as she momentarily forgot how to breathe.

Chapter 16

A black and white photo of Coit Tower starkly contrasted the upbeat magazines positioned on either side. Evie read the title of the article out loud, "Minor development in the mystery jumper from Coit Tower."

Evie's brows pulled together as she picked up the paper and inspected the story. Her eyes skimmed the first paragraph as her mind quickly grasped onto the fact that new security measures were apparently being put into place at the tower.

She was just about to turn the page to continue the story when a grumpy voice called, "No reading without buying."

The man at the counter had pulled off a single headphone and called out several decibels louder than necessary over the generous stacks of paper.

It took every ounce of willpower in Evie's body to refrain from rolling her eyes as she looked over at the stranger. She held his gaze for a moment and replied, "Fine."

Evie crossed the small distance to the counter and reached into her back pocket. She pulled out several crumpled bills. The man mumbled something unintelligible under his breath about credit cards as he grabbed the money and rubbed the bills against the corner of the counter in a weak attempt to straighten them out.

Evie watched the motions with a bored expression expertly plastered across her delicate features. Her catlike eyes took in the motion as she noticed the cluttered tattoos that spanned from the top of the younger man's fingers and disappeared underneath the material of his wrinkled shirt. A significant black swirl claimed the majority of his outer palm. The dark lines whirled around in a pattern that vaguely resembled a flattened image of an approaching tornado. A small white speck stood out against the contrasting obsidian.

"What's that?" Evie nudged her head in the direction of his hand.

The man momentarily stopped his fiddling with the dollar bills and followed Evie's gaze. He looked down at his hand and answered, "It's supposed to look like a hurricane. That little white dot symbolizes the eye of the storm. It means that there will always be a moment of peace before the end of a difficult journey. My girlfriend thinks that it means that if the first round of something bad didn't get you, then the second round will definitely try its hardest."

"Interesting." Evie wasn't exactly sure what to say as she clenched the newspaper a little tighter than needed under her arm.

The man kept messing with the money so Evie sighed and mumbled, "Keep the change."

She left the store and headed in the direction of her favorite rundown coffee shop for a cup of Joe that often burned the roof of her mouth. It wasn't exactly about the flavor, but more about the ambiance. The shop was one of the last few places in the city that Evie had attended with her parents. As a kid, Evie had loved getting the donuts and milk with her dad after a long day of class. Even though the shop was faded and the paint was a dull gray, it still reminded her of a long-forgotten home. Maybe, after all of this time, Evie was still chasing ghosts.

Chapter 17

"One cup of black coffee."

Evie pulled out another sparse wad of change and nodded in thanks as a paper cup was filled to the brim with dark steaming sludge. She nodded her head in thanks and then sat down at the counter.

Her fingers quickly opened the newspaper and a layer of ink and dirt stuck to the pads of her thumbs as she opened the pages. The scent of paper and ink filled Evie's senses. The smell battled against the formidable aroma of coffee for dominance.

Evie suspiciously searched around the tiny coffee shop as she tried to gauge the level of awareness in the room. Satisfied that the workers were busy and that the one customer in the corner was occupied, Evie pulled out a small flask from the inside of her sleeve. She poured in a generous shot or two and causally stirred the liquid with a wooden stirrer. She told herself that it was a proper Irish coffee. Part of her heritage. At least, on her father's side.

Eventually, the smell of coffee won and all other smells slowly faded into the background of Evie's awareness. Her gaze was too focussed on the lengthy news story to care. A flutter of excitement whirled in her chest as she realized that it was possible that this particular article held more information than the previous one.

Evie took a deep gulp of air and whispered the story out loud. Half of her could barely believe that such a break in her impromptu case was real. It was like a lead in the story had fallen right into her lap. Usually, she had to spend countless hours and sometimes even days looking for even the smallest clue. However, that was definitely not the case today as she read the last paragraph, "Mystery woman found dead at base of Coit Tower is officially ruled as a suicide. Friends and family of the deceased claim foul play. Mother of the young woman swears that her daughter was happy and full of life. Friends of the young woman claim that she had been experiencing stress and hormonal mood swings. Mental health is one of the leading problems facing young women today. If you need psychological assistance please get help or contact one of the local mental health hotlines."

A growing rage bubbled in the pit of Evie's belly. She closed the newspaper with such force that the pages crackled together like the snapping of a log. The people behind the register looked up at the sudden commotion, but Evie didn't pay them any mind. A red flush crept along her neck as she mulled over the words in the article.

"Telling a woman that she's just stressed is the modern version of calling a woman hysterical. What a cop out."

Pun intended.

Evie had stopped going to the doctors after she had been told one too many times that she was stressed. Yes, Evie had been stressed, but that had been a symptom not a cause. The last time that she had willingly gone was right after getting shot when working a case alongside Uncle Jack. The male physician that attended to her had said that her stress levels were to blame for feeling so sick. He hadn't even checked her for the infection that had been festering in her internal organs. The bullet wound had gotten infected. Of course, he had simply waved her off and told her to get some rest.

It wasn't relaxing to feel your organs slowly shutting down. That discovery had come a few days later when Evie had gotten so sick that she hadn't been able to get out of bed. If it wasn't for Jack rushing her to the hospital and swearing up and down for someone to give her a full examination, she'd likely already be six feet under.

The physical pain of the memory felt distant and dulled, but the emotional trauma still cut through Evie like a hot knife. There was a certain sense of betrayal that came with being disappointed by the people and system that was supposedly designed to protect you. It was a feeling that often stuck with Evie so often that it motivated her to go above and beyond when she accepted a case. She never wanted a stone to go unturned or a wrong to go unpunished. It wasn't fair to her clients if she just gave up. A sick sense of empathy had taken root after years of being fed by the blinding rays of disappointment.

Evie reached out and took a long sip of her coffee. She wanted a moment of peace within the chaos. Her eyes flitted over the story one more time as the image of Coit Tower stood out in black and white against the very front of the newspaper. Her mind returned back to the mention of a mother within the article. Evie decided that the scene of the crime was a good place to start. She hadn't ventured over to Telegraph Hill in a long while so there really was no time like the present to explore.

For once, Evie refrained from stomping her feet at the mere idea of leaving her favorite rundown coffeeshop. Instead, she slapped down a small tip and headed out to face the rest of her morning with an extremely misplaced sense of enthusiasm.

Chapter 18

The distance up Telegraph Hill had Evie's lungs burning. Each breath felt like a possible last. That was the price she paid for casually smoking half a pack of cigarettes on a near daily basis. Not that Evie had any intention of turning around her bad habits at a time like this.

Evie wheezed and slanted her body forward as her calves burned from exertion. A child zipped passed and giggled with glee. It took every ounce of willpower in Evie's body not to trip the little girl that carelessly trampled over Evie's shoes.

"It's just a kid. It's just a kid," The mantra did little to quell Evie's frazzled emotions as she reached the halfway point on the hill. Next time, she was coming from the opposite direction.

A bead of sweat trickled down Evie's brow as she pulled out her phone. She glanced at the lock screen and took a moment to check her texts on the sidewalk as her rapid breathing slowly came under control. Each deep gulp of air felt like an electric shock. Her wheezes and the sound of the occasional passing car were the only audible noises in the area.

Evie glanced up from her phone and took in the view. Buildings from below were scattered around like varied colorful leaves in the wind. The ocean was clear and bright as the sun danced along the moving surface. The scene looked like something from a postcard. In fact, Evie was relatively sure that a very similar view was on one of the multiple postcard options in the Coit Tower gift shop.

Slightly more energized, Evie locked her phone and slid it back into her pocket. Her knees burned from the activity, but Evie could finally see Coit Tower. She watched as several tourists snapped photos of the famous century-old landmark.

Evie eventually reached the base and stretched her legs on one of the surrounding patches of grass. Her eyes darted around as she tried to detect the scene of the crime. She wasn't sure why, but a part of her had childishly expected several chunks of bright yellow caution tape to encompass the entire area. Instead, people moved around and laughed with friends on picnic blankets as if nothing utterly malicious and completely diabolical had ever happened. The entire population seemed to be living in a reality completely alternate to Evie's.

Perplexed, she looked outward. The view of the city momentarily took Evie's mind away from the current chaos. Seagulls flew high and occasionally swooped down at random. Boats entered the harbor at leisure and the clear day allowed Evie a glimpse of Alcatraz. The long abandoned prison stood in the center of a small island. The snippet of land was completely surrounded by frigid water that possessed a hidden and unforgiving current. The water alone had made escape from the prison nearly impossible. The lurking danger of a formidable current combined with the otherworldly chilling water temperature to create a perilous situation.

Evie turned her attention back to Coit Tower and craned her head in a weak attempt to see. She squinted her eyes and placed her hand on her forehead. The effort made little difference and failed to shield her sensitive eyes from the unusually bright sun. It was typical that October and November were dreary months filled with a casual light cover of rain and fog. The marine layer often gave the city a quiet sleepy quality that felt at odds with the bustle and vigor of its constantly noisy inhabitants.

However, the view from Coit Tower stretched for miles. Evie could swear that she even noticed the slightest glimpse of houses from across the bay. The gulls called out from above as two young children scampered around a bright red picnic blanket.

The moment of peace felt completely at odds with the reason for Evie's visit. She looked at the tower as a blank stare took over her features. The joy experienced by the clueless strangers felt like a different reality from everything that Evie knew.

A woman had died here less than a week ago, but people walked around and carelessly strolled the grounds as if nothing had ever happened. Evie morbidly wondered if the bright red picnic blanket was randomly situated on top of the scene of the crime. The red of the fabric looked like a bright red bullseye.

Evie walked closer to the entrance of Coit Tower and caught a glimpse of the intricate artwork inside. The tower had been created in the early 1930s and artists from all over the city had come together to create a breathtaking canvas that portrayed city life during that time period.

A wealthy woman had given an extremely generous amount of money to the city of San Francisco on the condition that it be used to beautify and add value to the larger city. Now, almost 100 years later, Coit Tower still reigns supreme over Telegraph Hill with walls filled with colorful murals and priceless recordkeeping details as diligently portrayed by dozens of artists.

Evie had forgotten just how much she enjoyed exploring Coit Tower. She had found it to be one of her favorite places in the city when she was a child. Mainly, Evie had enjoyed it because most of her classmates had rarely ventured over to tourist attraction. They had remained safely sequestered into the finer restaurants or the planned visits to Alamo

Square Park. To Evie, the tower had been a source of refuge from a world that only knew her by name.

Growing up, Evie hadn't tasted a desperate hunger for solitude. That came later. At night, Evie could sometimes hear the screeching of metal in the back of her mind. The clanging of plastic and glass as it pounded against the ground. Evie inhaled sharply and headed into Coit Tower.

She didn't intend to stay long, but the opportunity was just too fortunate to miss. She wandered the halls and stood a few feet away from the murals. Evie was afraid that even a heavy breeze would rip off some sections of the painted walls. It was evident that there had been some restoration efforts over the years, but how long could such priceless paintings hold up against the constant onslaught of time combined with the unforgiving ocean air?

Evie looked up and wondered if the city would eventually need to invest in a sturdier boundary to separate the public from the walls or at least break down and purchase a better ventilation system. The tower wasn't likely to receive heavy financial backing unless advocated for by the public. Luckily, San Francisco seemed to be the roosting place for many beloved artists and authors. It seemed likely that the tower had a chance to stand another 50 years to even 100 years with such passionate backers of the arts.

A mural caught Evie's attention as she slowly rounded the corner. The image portrayed a car accident in the center of a bustling city street. Several onlookers stood close to the sidewalk as the police arrived and tried to sort out the scene. Near the center of the painting and somewhat second to the accident, stood a man with his arms away from his body. A shady individual was robbing the man in broad daylight thanks to the chaos created by the wreck.

The artists of the time had placed a few Easter eggs within their works. They had managed to encompass more aspects of San Francisco than likely originally intended by the city.

These artists had been bold in their quest to offer a more realistic image of the truth. They had taken that saying about pictures being worth a 1,000 words to heart and attempted to explain everything in detail to anyone willing to take the time and observe.

Evie's pace faltered as she once again admired the broad brush strokes and wide faces. It was obvious in some areas where different artists had taken over certain sections. The art told a comprehensive story that had been broken down into small, but engaging chunks. The unity of the work spoke of an overlap between individualism and collective pride. An overlap that seemed to be so clearly defined and so often isolated less than 100 years later.

Today, that sense of hometown pride seemed to be missing. At least, it was missing for Evie.

She raised her hands and ghosted the outline of a pale and somewhat ashen face. Not touching, but still lingering. Her fingers invisibly traced the outline with a reverence. It was as if the action alone could retrace the steps of the dead.

Chapter 19

The faded paint along the walls told a story about San Francisco that was just out of reach from common memory. Older cities tended to have long memories that stretched back generations. The collective memories were dipped in love and sprinkled with personality. For the violently conquered Wild West, San Francisco was easily one of the oldest cities. However, the memory of the city didn't stretch back even half as far as its European and Asian sister cities. It was simply too new. A century to a city in Europe or Asia was simply a handful of years. In contrast, a century was a priceless nugget of precious time for a windy city located along the Pacific Ocean.

Conveniently, San Francisco's collective memory had forgotten the tribes and thousands of people that had first held claim to the land. Sometimes, memories failed on purpose, especially when the truth was too uncomfortable for the writers of popularly accepted history books.

Fortunately, artists even loyal to such cities often remained true to a different code.

Evie's pale fingers ghosted over the image of a man. He remained painted with his hand permanently outstretched, reaching for a work by Karl Marx. A pleased smile prodded at the corner of Evie's mouth as she took in the sly detail. Her eyes momentarily sparkled with mischief and understanding. It seemed that artists had always pushed the envelope against authority in one way or another. Fighting a soundless battle to accurately represent the voices often silenced by powerful leaders.

Suddenly, a small folded scrap of paper caught Evie's eyes. The paper was neatly rolled and tucked just a few inches away from the man reaching for Marx. Without thinking, Evie plucked the paper from its hidden position in the wall. Paranoid, she glanced around and noticed that the rest of the crowd was still none the wiser. Parents cluelessly explored the room as they followed behind their children. The simple actions provided a sense of normalcy. The sight settled Evie's nerves, but her fingers still shook. She tried to shake the tension from her shoulders. Evie unrolled the paper and squinted at the messy scrawling penmanship. The handwritten note conveyed a sense of urgency.

Evie hesitated, but then she licked her lower lip and read, "If you're reading this then I never left Coit Tower. He made me disappear from memory. Please make sure that I'm not forgotten."

The note abruptly ended and a shiver raced down the entire length of Evie's spine. She felt as if someone had just walked over her grave. The note was the very first sign that Evie wasn't insane. She clenched the paper within her hands as if the words were liable to fly off the page and disappear from sight at any given second.

Chapter 20

The articles had given Evie hope and the newly discovered handwritten letter had provided her with faith. The murdered woman had existed. After so many hours of self doubt, Evie finally knew that she was real. The unknown woman had likely stumbled onto some extremely sensitive information.

It was a massive stretch, but Evie was pretty sure that with enough time, she'd be able to find the mother from the newspaper article. Somehow, the sparse information and thin clues had led Evie on a wild goose chase just a few blocks away from her own apartment. However, that wasn't much of a surprise. Women seemed to disappear at a much faster rate in Evie's neighborhood when compared to other parts of the city. It wasn't completely unsurprising, given that people with less resources made easier prey. It was much simpler to make a person disappear when they had limited access to money or power. The bleak understanding twisted an invisible blade deeper into Evie's chest.

She tried to dispel her darker and more morbid thoughts as they scampered around in the back of her mind like rats in a cellar.

Suddenly, a dog barked with such ferocity that Evie stirred from her thoughts and looked around. A hoarse laugh escaped Evie's chapped lips as she looked at the culprit. The mutt scampered behind the glass window of a dressmaker's shop and furiously barked at every person that dared to walk near his domain. The small dog bounced from one end of the shop window to the other as he vigilantly chased behind potential troublemakers that dared get too close to his territory. His tail was stiff and alert as he bared his tiny canines.

"Don't worry, Napoleon. You'll be fine." Evie wasn't exactly sure of the dog's actual name, but the description seemed to fit. Evie trailed down the street and the yapping grew distant.

She glanced to the right and stopped as soon as she noticed a forlorn woman stooped over in a diner. Her defeated body language was easily visible from the outside of the shop.

Usually, Evie was the first one to actively ignore another person's discomfort. She often tried to provide the other individual with a sense of privacy. It felt wrong to pry when someone was obviously going through something. Especially, when it was a stranger. For some reason, Evie decided to be nosy.

The gut feeling didn't make any sense, but it was possibly the best hunch that she had had since the start of her impromptu investigation.

The woman's features looked defeated as her shoulders hunched down. Her head remained lowered like a flag at half mast. The sight of the older woman easily drew Evie in as she pulled open the door and sat on a stool directly to the stranger's right.

Evie kept her gaze glued to the street as she tried to gauge the woman's emotions from the edges of her vision. The task felt nearly impossible, but Evie refused to make the other woman suspicious of her intentions.

Eventually, Evie drew in a deep breath and asked, "Long day?"

The question sounded beyond idiotic, even to Evie's ears. Half of her wanted to pound her face against the window and claim insanity. After so many years working with people, Evie still seemed to be more than a little green when it came to handling painful emotions.

"Long month."

Surprise momentarily colored Evie's features at the other woman's open reply. She weighed her options and decided that there was no perfect way to begin the conversation.

"How so?"

The other woman drew a careless pattern on the bartop counter. Her finger drifted and circled around a spot of ketchup before she retracted the digit closer to her body and traced along the edge of the table.

"I feel like I'm in a dream and I can't wake up. This is the worst nightmare that I've ever had and there is no way out."

Bingo. Evie had a feeling that her gut and impromptu online searches had brought her to the right person. The content had been sparse, but Evie had patched it together.

"I saw the articles about your daughter and I want to help."

The sentence had the other woman recoiling as if Evie had threatened to burn down her house. The stranger's jaw slackened as her eyes turned guarded. Her once casual demeanor had hardened into an icy shell.

Alarmed, Evie quickly tried to backtrack and thaw out the situation. She added, "I want to help. I want to get justice for your daughter."

"You can't. It would be better for you if you just got up now and left. You have no idea the kind of murky water that you're swimming in, Little Lady."

"Then help me to understand. If you want any chance at getting justice for your daughter then I am your best shot."

The older woman turned in her seat and fully regarded Evie. She inspected Evie from head to toe before her tired eyes finally settled on Evie's confident gaze. Evie silently implored the woman to confide in her. The articles had left Evie haunted. She couldn't even begin to fathom what this poor mother was feeling. Evie knew that she'd continue investigating even without the mother's cooperation. The story had made her feel obsessed.

"Evangeline was a sweet girl. She had so much life and promise, but then she ended up hanging out with the wrong crowd. She came home drunk and high more often than not. Evangeline then started stealing from me. At first, a few dollars here or there, but then jewelry started going missing and it all became too much. I kicked her out and instantly regretted it. When I finally tracked her down and had asked her to come home, she had refused. She was acting paranoid and at the time, I had thought that it was the drugs, but now I know better. Someone had been following her. I failed her."

Evie wasn't sure what to say. Words were often too cheap to compensate for grief. Evie watched the older woman as she drowned within her deep despair.

After a minute, Evie implored, "Let me help."

Evangeline's mom gave Evie an odd look. It was something that emulated grief, but didn't exactly capture the same heartfelt expression. In the blink of an eye, the glance disappeared.

"I'll tell you what I know, but it isn't much."

Evie sighed, "It's a start."

Friday

November 1st of 2019

Chapter 21

"Here you go, Kid. The finest cake this side of the Golden Gate Bridge."

Jack brought over a vanilla flavored cake with buttercream frosting. It had the visual likeness of cellophane with a chalky taste that was just about two steps above what was offered in every value-brand supermarket. It was heaven.

Evie choked back a wave of emotion as it threatened to crash onto her thin shoulders. She touched her fingers to her mouth as her lips quivered with uncertainty.

"I would have told the waiters, but the idea of having all of them coming over to sing about your birthday sounded more like a punishment."

"Thanks, Jack."

"Anytime, Kid. It's not every day that you turn 28."

Evie looked up at Jack and noticed the heavy circles that clung beneath his eyes. He had insisted on taking Evie out for an early lunch even though he had just finished a grueling shift less than an hour before. Jack often spent his nights investigating the missing cases and traveling from one section of the city to the next.

"So what did you tell them?"

"Huh?"

"How did you explain buying a small cake at eleven in the morning?"

"Oh, that." Jack sliced his hand through the air with the same vigor as someone waving away a pestilent fly. He settled back into his chair and the material of his white wrinkled button-down shirt strained against his belly.

Jack looked over at Evie and gave her one of his rare mysterious smiles which were only reserved for his family members. The grins usually appeared when talking with his two sons. The little male trio were known for sneaking out of the house and going on late night snack runs after staying up too late watching cheesy reruns of bad cop television shows.

"I said that you'd gotten a promotion. Before you say it's a blatant lie, that's wrong. In a way, you were promoted to a new age group and that's the official story that we're sticking with."

A pleased smile tugged at the corner of Evie's lips as she nudged an empty small plate to Jack's side of the table. Jack grabbed it and placed it next to his large soda and coffee.

She mumbled. "You're the boss."

Jack yawned, "Only when it comes to murder and cake."

"What a spread."

Jack cut two generous slices of cake as he said, "It's important to have range, Kid."

He slid the larger slice of cake in Evie's direction and then placed a generous helping of frosted chemical waste onto his own plate.

The spoon looked absolutely doll-like next to Evie's ginormous helping. Jack had given her a slice that took up nearly the entire plate.

For a moment, Evie quietly chewed a large bite. The artificially flavored icing melted against her tongue. Evie preferred the overly sweet frosting and enjoyed the extremely processed taste. She nibbled against the corner of the spoon like a worried hamster.

Jack glanced up and noticed her odd behavior. He released a loud sigh, "Okay, out with it. What's on your mind? You haven't even started your second piece and you never leave any survivors with this sugar-packed monstrosity. It's DeLucca's Delights, your favorite place in town. Don't tell me that's changed."

A small frown crossed Jack's features at the thought. He looked like a worried mother hen as he glanced between Evie's barely touched slice of cake and her face.

"That's not it. The cake is still delicious," Evie paused as she struggled to collect her thoughts.

She wasn't sure how to bring up the newspaper article again in a way that didn't sound obsessed. However, the possibility that Jack had found information about the case was just too good to ignore. Evie narrowed her eyes and decided to jump right in. Well, after a generous spoonful of cake. The fake frosting tasted like sweet sidewalk chalk and Evie found that the familiar flavor managed to settle some of her nerves.

"I'm still thinking about the woman that died earlier this week in Telegraph Hill."

In less than a second, Jack's posture changed from that of a relaxed and exhausted uncle to a seasoned detective in one of the largest cities in the world. Jack's gaze turned hard and all of his previous warmth cooled into a tepid analytical gaze.

"I told you to drop it."

Jack leaned over the table and added, "I did some digging and there wasn't even a police report that mentioned a death on Telegraph Hill. Not for the entire week.

The news instantly stoked the embers of Evie's curiosity as her eyes turned bright with excitement. She tried to keep her composure, but Jack easily noticed the change in her demeanor.

He slammed a frustrated palm down against the wood veneered table. Glasses and plates rattled at the sudden impact. A few droplets of coffee dribbled down the side of Evie's mug.

Jack's gaze looked almost pleading as he implored, "You don't understand, Evie. Cases like these don't just fully disappear from the record. Evidence might go missing or details in files might be changed, courtesy of a dirty cop, but never completely wiped away. This smells to high heaven."

"But that's good! That means that we are on the right path."

"Evie Laythorne, you leave this alone. This case is not your problem. Don't go looking for this type of trouble because you probably won't come back. Do you understand?"

Evie felt something close to rage as she glanced at Jack's pinched features. She took a moment to look at Jack and really saw the truth. Underneath his stern words and unnecessary table pounding was a man with few verbal tools; desperate to make a point. He wasn't mad. Worse, Jack was terrified for her safety.

She reached across the table and gave one of Jack's fisted palms a gentle squeeze. Evie looked up and desperately tried to convey the emotions behind her eyes with a single look. She wanted Jack to know that she appreciated everything that he had done for her.

"I know you're scared, Jack."
"Don't start this with me, Evie. You have no right putting your nose in places where it doesn't belong."
"That's ironic coming from a lead detective."

Evie leaned back and petulantly folded her arms over her chest as she tried to keep warm. Her mind wandered to the recently murdered Golden Gate psychopath.

Evie looked around the small diner. It had a sparse collection of available pastry items in the brightly illuminated glass case. The cakes were small and mostly multi-colored, but Evie had no interest in that anymore. She glanced down at the still unfinished cake at their table and instead reached for her cup of coffee. Evie took a sip and the bitter taste caused her lips to curl in distaste.

She knew that she'd made an error. A fatal action in her nearly perfect performance. Evie pretended to look at the other people in the restaurant as sweat trickled down the side of her neck.

"What's in the cup, Kid?"
Jack wasn't asking. It was more of a knowing statement than anything else.

Evie swallowed a bit of spit and blew out a breath away from Jack's face. She deadpanned, "Coffee."

"And?"

"It's an Irish coffee. I'm going back to my roots for this birthday." Evie slipped into a more frigid demeanor as if daring Jack to disagree.

She said it with such ease that it was almost like pulling on a sweater. Typical.

However, the change in her tone gave Jack a moment to pause. He looked deep into Evie's eyes and held her gaze. The intensity and concern behind his stare was too much and Evie quickly looked away. She grabbed her cup and busied herself with the nonexistent task of cleaning the spilled coffee from the side of her mug. Evie reached over and rubbed away a few spots of the spilt beverage from the fake wood.

She had mentally prepared for this inevitable conversation with Jack at least a hundred times. Evie thought that she had been so careful. She had even arrived at the diner a few minutes before Jack just so that she could order her coffee and discretely pour the contents of her flask into the half-emptied mug. Unfortunately, the contrast between unreasonably sweet cake and bottom shelf whiskey had proven to be an error. Rookie mistake.

"It's like I'm looking at a ghost."

Now it was Evie's turn to be confused as she clarified, "What?"

Jack sighed, "You might be here with me in this diner, but it's not really you. You're not really here with me, Kid."

Evie tried to make a joke to dispel the tension, but her actions fell short. She prodded, "What do you mean? I'm right next to you."

"No, Evie. Sometimes I think that you never really left that car accident. It's like you're sitting in the car and refusing to get out. I can't go over and grab you and no one else can pull you out. It's a place that you have to leave on your own. Right now, I'm seeing a ghost more than I'm seeing you."

"That's a nice birthday speech."

Jack leaned back against his chair, defeated by Evie's intentionally flippant comment. He gripped the spoon so tightly that Evie swore that any more force would cause it to snap in half like a twig. He leveled Evie with a gaze that struck her to the core.

Jack kept the spoon in an inescapable deathgrip. He pleaded, "Just make sure that you find your way home, Kid."

Saturday

November 2nd of 2019

Chapter 22

Most days tended to be quiet in the apartment complex, but not Saturdays. Saturdays were full of giggling children that rose early enough to see the sun climb into the sky as the smell of freshly ground coffee wafted through the walls. Old latin love songs drifted along the static-filled air waves and willed the world into existence. On Saturdays and only on Saturdays, Evie enjoyed staying in bed a little longer than usual. The anxiety and weight that often pulled at her heart was kept at a distance thanks to a healthy dose of second-hand connection. The sounds that echoed through the thin walls and clambered through the old pipes enveloped Evie in a sense of belonging, if only for a few minutes.

The sun climbed higher into the sky like a child swinging on a jungle gym. Eventually the cheery rays stood eye level with Evie's bed. She sighed and slunk away from the threadbare sheets. Her sandals shuffled into the tiny kitchen. Evie blindly reached into the breadbox and yelped. A sharp throbbing pain emanated from the tip of her finger. Bright red blood dribbled from the cut as Evie opened the breadbox door a little wider.

Hesitantly, she peaked inside and groaned, "Well, hello there, Little Guest."

A small mouse hid near the back of the wooden box, just behind a nearly empty bottle of vodka. Large bright eyes blinked up at Evie and managed to quell the heartbeat that now pulsed at the tip of her finger.

"Hold still. I need to find some tupperware."

Evie wiggled the bloodied finger in the mouse's direction for emphasis. She ripped open a cupboard that was stuffed with pots and pans.

"I swear that Jack gave me tupperware. It has to be here. It's not like any of it has ever been used." Evie turned over a large pot as several tupperware containers and lids toppled to the ground.

Prepared for battle, Evie held the plastic container in one hand and carefully opened the breadbox with the other. A brave little warrior was prepared for battle. However, Evie was actually playing the unpopular role of Goliath.

Suddenly, a ball of fur bounced and squeaked from one section of the box to the other. Oddly enough, Evie found her panic rising with every tail twitch that skittered along the exposed skin of her wrist. Even a robber with a gun had failed to elicit such a strong emotion. Evie decided that it was the odd sensation of the thin tail as it swept along her skin which incited inner turmoil. The sensation wasn't unpleasant, but it was still unsettling. Like bumping into something soft and unexpected inside of a dark room.

Another squeak drew Evie back to the moment as she quickly placed the container over the little mouse and effectively left it trapped.

"Now you're stuck, Little Critter. Don't worry."

Evie gingerly slid the lid underneath the tiny mouse's feet and secured the tupperware locks. She barely managed to grab the keys to the front door. Her gaze never left the dark onyx eyes of the mouse. She hastily locked the door and cautiously walked down the narrow winding staircase.

"Please don't chew the plastic. Please don't bite me, again. I really like having all of my digits in place when lighting a cigarette. How about this, I'll put you outside and then it's a win-win situation. Does that sound good?"

Intelligent beady eyes blinked twice and Evie accepted the action as confirmation. Good. She had a deal with a mouse.

Bright sunshine pounded into Evie's skull. She squinted and walked several paces away from the building. She wanted to make sure that her new tiny friend didn't get any ideas about returning. The gesture was worth a try. After all, the little guy was now the first pet that Evie had ever owned.

"Okay, time to go."

Evie unlocked the lid and waited as the small creature tentatively crept out. After a few seconds of indecision, it sped across the ground and took cover underneath a clearly abandoned car. One wheel was stripped bare of rubber and the rest of the wheels were heavily deflated. At least, there was little danger that the tiny mouse's cover would suddenly turn on and drive away.

"Bye, Buddy. Hopefully we don't meet again." Evie gave the creature a lazy wave and turned to head inside.

Several rambunctious cat calls from a few feet away drew Evie's attention. Her cool stare landed on three disheveled men. They were hunched over a bartop table outside of a neighborhood supermarket as they hooted and hollered. One of them kept his mouth agape as if he needed too many brain cells to breathe through his nose and harass women at the same time. The tasteless behavior wasn't anything new to Evie, but she found it too early in the morning to tolerate. Besides, she already did her good deed for the day, right?

The long nightshirt was several sizes too large, but it still clung to her figure and rode up her pale thighs as she stood up from her previously crouched position. Evie's eyes were honed in on her prey. To stir the pot, Evie added a stereotypical sashay to her hips as she walked over to the low lives. The men grew louder and they reminded Evie of stray dogs when strangers drew too close. Except, these dogs likely had both bite and bark. Today, that didn't bother Evie. She didn't mind that they were loud because they appeared equally just as stupid. Evie smelt the cheap liquor as it wafted from their clothes. It hinted at the fact that they were still out from the night before.

"Do you have a light?"

Evie's voice took on a deeper, throaty quality as she asked the question and popped her hip.

Unsurprisingly, Evie's question caught the men off-guard. It was almost as if their aggressive cat calling had never previously garnered a positive reaction.

Groundbreaking.

Seeing as the group likely didn't care about comfort or consent, Evie had a feeling that they often cat called and degraded little girls that had physically matured early. To them, the city was their playground. All things up for grabs.

With great care, Evie kept her face passive as she swayed closer. Once she was less than a few feet away from the man that stood closest to her, she waited. The semi-circle of toxic-masculinity waited for their unofficial leader to make the first move.

Bored, Evie asked again, but at a much slower pace, "Do you have a smoke?"

Hands instantly delved into pockets. The guy on the right even turned his pockets inside and out during his frantic search. His wayward hair flopped into his eyes as less than half of it remained in its previously gelled position.

"Here." The man in a gold necklace with a worn wife beater offered a standard lighter that came in those classic packs of four at the gas station.

"Thanks." Evie leaned over and took in several deep inhales from the new cigarette. The flame at the base of the cigarette grew redder with every inhale. Eventually, Evie released the smoke from within her chest and wisps of gray trailed into the morning air. The nicotine tasted lighter than her usual preference, but Evie figured she wasn't in a position to be picky when she was mainly taking a cigarette to prove a point. A very unhinged point, but still. Even for Evie, smoking before ten in the morning felt wrong. Likely because her stomach still had a few lingering remains of wine from the night before.

"What brings you over here, Fancy Bitch?"

The man on the right licked his lips and leered at Evie. His gaze traveled from her half-painted toe nails to her disheveled hair.

Instead of answering, Evie took in another drag from her cigarette as her gaze remained passive. Her silence drifted on and the men around her shuffled and scratched at their beards as if she had no choice in the world, but to answer. It was as if the group was convinced that the term you can run, but you can't hide, also applied to responding to men.

Bored, Evie turned around and prepared to leave the little circle. Suddenly, the man that had so dutifully turned his pockets inside and out to search for a lighter grew angry. His features turned harsh as a large hand shot out and roughly gripped Evie's bicep. The pressure hurt as the man squeezed her flesh as if he was intending to teach her a lesson.

"Answer him, bitch. You're being rude. Besides, you owe us that much for the smoke. We went through a lot of effort to help you."

Evie tilted her head as a lopsided grin crept along her features. She looked at the group as her smile turned from mildly pleased to that of an unhinged child on Christmas morning.

She took another unhurried drag of the cigarette and then pressed the butt into the center of the hand that held her captive. A yelp resounded around the street as the creep pulled his hand back to his chest. The group looked utterly confused as they stared between Evie and their injured friend. The dots seemed nearly impossible for them to connect. More likely, they refused to believe that the dots could possibly be connected.

Evie pulled a face once she noticed that the bottom of her cigarette had bent in the process. Guess her smoke break was over.

Before any of the group had processed what had happened, Evie sauntered over to the entrance of her apartment building. She kept the ruined cigarette clamped firmly between her lips. Curses and shouts followed, but Evie paid them no attention as she retrieved the cigarette from her mouth and flicked it in the general direction of the group. Her eyes locked with the man that still held his burnt hand as if he had just returned from war. Pleased, Evie sent him a wink and then unlocked the heavy metallic door as her slim frame slipped inside. The words, "You have a death wish, lady!" Swung around the hinges and made it into the stairwell with Evie.

Fluorescent lights flickered and the concrete shone against the yellow-tinted light. A security camera in the corner remained trained on the door, but Evie knew that it had broken two summers ago and that the building management hadn't noticed or cared to fix it. Its large telescopic eye looked at Evie and captured her in its unblinking stare. For some, just its presence was a deterrent, but for others whether the camera worked or failed wasn't even a consideration. It was the committed ones that unnerved Evie.

She waved at the large eye and then leisurely walked up the stairs. She took each step with unhurried strides. The thrill from only a few minutes ago, already gone.

Her fingers gripped the small apartment key and a sigh of relief left her previously pursed lips. For a moment, Evie had feared that she had dropped her keys outside. She reached out to insert the key into the lock, but stopped short.

The door was open just wide enough so that Evie could see inside. Unsure if she had locked the door in her haste to kick out her new roommate, Evie stood outside. She wiped her sweaty palms down the sides of the oversized shirt and made up her mind. She pushed open the door and quickly jumped to the side.

Her eyes anxiously scanned the small room for even the slightest hint of an intruder. Luckily, the room was so small that she could see from her tiny bed all the way to the kitchen without even needing to move from the entry. Evie scanned the room a second time and realized that she couldn't see inside of her tiny bathroom. It was so small that at times, Evie brushed her shoulders against the wall or stubbed her toe against the bathtub when she was getting changed.

Cautiously, Evie crept into her kitchen and grabbed a blade. It was a slim steak knife, but it was still a better weapon than nothing. Armed with a value-brand knife and a missing amount of self-preservation, Evie kicked open the bathroom door.

Chapter 23

Nothing.

The empty room mocked Evie's sense of paranoia. She could have sworn that someone had been in her studio. It was a strong feeling deeply settled into Evie's chest. The rumpled towel was still casually thrown over the shower rack. It was exactly as she had left it. Her toothbrush still precariously balanced on the edge of the sink. Surely an intruder would have knocked it off.

"You okay, Mijita?" An older feminine voice called out from the hallway.

Evie turned around and noticed her kind elderly neighbor from across the hall. The older woman held up an umbrella between her weathered hands. It diligently shook within her grasp, but remained raised high above her head like a makeshift baseball bat. Her brown eyes that had lightened over time, glanced suspiciously around the room. Age would never touch her indomitable spirit.

For a moment, Evie felt sorry for the potential intruder. She took a step out of the bathroom so that she could speak with her sweet neighbor.

"Hi, Mrs. Flores. Everything is fine. I thought someone was in the bathroom, but apparently that's not the case." Evie gave a wide gesture to the bathroom and then gestured to the kitchen with the hand that was still holding a knife.

Mrs. Flores's gaze landed on the knife and she arched one thin brown brow in maternal disapproval. Slowly, her shaking arms lowered. The bottom of the umbrella landed with a light thud on the ground.

She smacked her lips, "You need something better to protect yourself. You are much too flaquita to go around with just a knife, blindly hoping for the best. You need a metal-tipped umbrella to do the trick. It's never failed me in 86 years." Mrs. Flores tapped the ground with the lowered end of her umbrella for added emphasis. After a moment, she said, "It's sturdy. Wait, I have another one in my apartment that you can keep. Let me go get it for you."

As Mrs. Flores turned to leave, Evie called out, "Don't worry, Mrs. Flores. I'll go and get one tomorrow. Thank you for coming to make sure that I'm okay."

Mrs. Flores gave an impish smile that stretched the fine lines of her tanned skin. She looked radiant as something similar to a halo encircled the top of her neatly braided hair. She crooned, "Of course, Niña. Always happy to help. Besides, us ladies need to stick together." She gave Evie a motherly nod and then turned away. Evie watched until the older woman closed and locked her door. With a sigh, Evie walked over and decided to do the same.

The interaction quelled Evie's nerves and she double-checked the locks above her door before padding into the center of her studio. She looked at the sun as it proudly glimmered in the sky. Evie decided that it was time to get dressed.

After changing, Evie noticed the gun that she had confiscated from Mrs. Haversham. It was hidden under the sweater that Evie had tossed into the corner of the tiny broom-sized closet the night before. She stared at it for a moment. She contemplated keeping it hidden away. Making sure that it was hidden from use. A momentary recollection of the morning had her fingers instantly reaching out and enveloping the cool metallic handle. She lifted up the edge of her shirt and tucked the gun into the back of her pants.

Evie had never felt the need to have a gun. In fact, she had often complained to Jack about how unnecessary and dangerous they were in a nation dictated by greed instead of compassion. A place where every Tom, Dick, and Harry could get their hands on a death machine faster than applying for a car loan. She ranted on a near daily basis to Jack. He often retorted that although things had changed, they were still living in the Wild West. He claimed that technology had quickly outmatched the learning curve that people could process. Doomed to make expedited bad decisions. Evie didn't consider herself a Tom or a Harry, but she absolutely felt like a Dick. The gun pressed against her back as Evie desperately searched for a distraction.

A shiver ran down Evie's spine as she tried to ignore the weight of her decision. Eventually, she headed to the kitchen. She wondered if the cupboards had any mouse-proof food options. The odds were slim.

Her gaze settled on a half-full glass of whisky that sat next to the sink. Evie's brows drew together as she tried to remember the last time that she had ever failed to get to the bottom of a drink.

Chapter 24

Evie had a rough idea that some very powerful people were in play. Even in San Francisco, it took more than a little elbow grease to get rid of someone. Making someone disappear faster than morning fog on a sweltering summer day took work. It also took a ton of money.

Her thoughts jumbled together as she headed over to Jack's precinct. She knew that Jack usually took his lunch break at noon in the tiny donut shop across the street. Which was exactly why she had waited until ten minutes passed the hour to enter. She glanced around at the beat cops and a handful of rowdy suspects. Most of the people that worked in the building knew her after so many years of scampering around Jack's coat tails.

A woman in her late 50s sat behind the front desk. She lifted up her head at the sound of an approaching visitor. Her aged eyes brightened once they landed on Evie. She gave a friendly wave and chirped, "Hi, Evie! It's good to see you. How is everything?"

Warm brown eyes peered at Evie from behind thick glasses. The eyeglasses were easily two sizes too large for her petite features.

Unwilling to get caught in small talk, but also not wanting to be mean, Evie called back, "Good! Just between cases right now. I'm getting into one as we speak, Sylvie."

It was a half-truth. A silly statement closer to the truth than the woman behind the desk likely knew.

Sylvie's eyes comically widened with curiosity as she chomped into a chocolate glazed donut and asked, "Anything exciting?"

"Not sure. I'll tell you all about it later." Evie navigated around the front desk and headed in the direction of Jack's office.

Just then, a large man with tattoos up and down his arms entered the precinct. The ink sprawled all the way to his face where it ended in random collections of words and cartoons. He was placed between two officers that looked barely able to hold him. The man grew agitated as he spit and threw back his head in a fit of rage. The back of his skull crashed into an officer's nose. A sickening crack filled the air as several officers released impressive long-winded strings of curses. The commotion told Evie that it was her cue to leave the area.

Evie moved around the tiled hallways relatively unnoticed. The department knew her as Jack's unofficial daughter and she knew the department as the place where she had spent countless hours pouring over homework. To Evie, it didn't feel like a particularly fair trade. She still hated creative writing.

Finally, Evie slipped into Jack's office. Not much had changed since her last visit. She noticed the stacks of paperwork in precise order and saw the color-coded notes that poked around the edges of the formidable piles. Jack insisted on making copies of most case documents. He swore that holding the information in his hands helped him to put together clues faster.

Evie loved to give him grief about the environmentally wasteful process, but she begrudgingly wondered if there was an actual method to his madness. Afterall, he was the most known and respected detective in the Bay Area with a record of accomplishments that stretched longer than some discount supermarket receipts.

Of course, Evie hadn't snuck into Jack's office to reminisce. She was looking for clues about the missing woman that Jack had so passionately warned her to ignore. She knew that there was no way Jack planned to hand over any information on the subject. Especially not to her.

Luckily, Evie didn't need to creep around Jack's desk for long. She glanced at the screen and noticed that it was locked. A very angry looking Bald Eagle glared down at Evie from the computer's profile icon.

"Typical."

It wasn't that Evie didn't know Jack's password. In true Jack form, he hadn't bothered to update it in over a decade. It was still his wife's first name and the year that they had first gone on a date to the botanical garden. If anything went wrong, she didn't want to leave behind any time stamps or search logs. The computers were all visible to the main system which offered Evie little privacy if she planned to snoop around.

Evie's gaze flitted down to a desk calendar. The corner of her lip tilted up in appreciation as she noticed that Jack had placed her birthday in large blocky writing and then had circled it multiple times.

A piece of paper poked out just behind the flat calendar and Evie swiftly pulled at the corner. The white sheet was about the size of a standard piece of printer paper. The document was a typed list that included potential people and sources that Jack had somehow associated with the mystery woman. The names meant nothing to Evie, but she decided that wasn't anything that a quick search on the internet couldn't fix. She snapped a photo with her phone and then swiftly placed the paper back under the calendar where she had found it.

Suddenly, the handle to Jack's office jiggled. Evie held her breath and prepared to get caught. She knew that her current situation looked pretty damning. She rushed to find a likely excuse. Could she claim that she was just visiting?

However, Jack didn't enter. Instead, a young man no older than late twenties entered with a handful of papers. The jaunt in his step told Evie that he was still painfully new to the department.

His head was shoved into the content of the file as he said, "Hey, Detective Jack. I've printed out all of the info that I could find on the lead suspect, but I'm not sure that it will help."

After a brief pause, he glanced up and noticed Evie.

Chapter 25

"Who are you?" The handsome young man pulled the previously extended files closer to his body. He glared at Evie in a way that might have seemed intimidating at one point or another. However, the reaction simply caused Evie to grin.

Clearly, that wasn't the reaction that the young man had anticipated as he drew back his shoulders and took a step closer.

"You must be new here." Evie slid around Jack's massive desk as the information that she had so desperately needed remained safely hidden inside of her phone. She matched the young man's movements and drew back her own shoulders so that her frame looked taller, but still absolutely unimposing.

Evie stopped just a few inches away from the visibly tense stranger. He lowered his fingers and imperceptibly touched the top of his holstered gun. The warning was clear and Evie knew better than to push her luck. Especially when she had a loaded firearm stuffed down the back of her pants in the middle of a cop's playground. The last thing she wanted was to create a shootout over Jack's precious piles of notes. He'd definitely shoot someone for that.

Friendly department or not, the facts were not going to paint Evie in a flattering light if the new kid discovered the gun that she had placed in the back of her pants. She decided that the man with deep brown eyes had to be relatively fresh in the department to react so nervously to an unfamiliar face. Veterans of the department were relatively unphased by almost anything and everything. They all looked as impassive as stone.

But then again, Evie only knew what Jack had allowed her to see in the department and a jumpy newbie definitely wasn't on the list of mandatory sights.

She tried to recall if Jack had spoken about anyone new in his department. Her body language remained casual as she forced every muscle in her body to stay visibly relaxed. The last thing that Uncle Jack needed was a bloodied mess all over his carefully organized documents.

Unfortunately, Jack rarely spoke in detail about his job after hours. He had made it a point to leave it all at the door unless it was absolutely necessary. Evie tried to remember what Jack had mentioned the week before when they were seated at the tiny diner just outside of the Financial District. He had been speaking through a meatball sandwich and most of it had sounded like complaints about an eager, but relatively skeptical newbie. The newbie's name eluded Evie, but she decided that she didn't really need it.

She tilted her head to the side, "You're the newbie that's eager, but still totally skeptical about how much good he can do. Did I miss anything?" Evie internally cringed at her own voice. She felt like a first-rate pier fortune teller as she intentionally used vague blanket statements. Luckily, vague statements with a contradictory edge tended to apply to most people. Evie just hoped that the statement worked to win over the man that currently blocked her one and only escape route.

A brief pause told Evie that the words had hit their mark. A deep frown pulled between the man's thick brows. He glanced at Evie as if he was just seeing her for the first time.

"Who are you?"

"A friend of the department. Why are you in Jack's office?" Evie decided to turn the tables and go on the offensive.

"Classified."

"Not really."

"Why"

"You basically offered me those files only a few seconds ago. Clearly, they don't mean that much to you if you're letting just any person touch them."

A flushed tint appeared on the nape of the man's neck. With every second, the blush crept higher up his flushed skin. He sucked in a deep breath. His thin chest puffed out with displeasure. A muscle in his jaw clicked as he countered, "Not just anyone. I wanted to give them to Jack."

Evie quickly cut him off and countered, "Do you just address all of your superiors so casually or are you trying to disregard his ranking? Jack won't like this."

The trick question caught him off balance. It provided Evie with the perfect distraction. She circled around the desk. He had unwittingly followed Evie as she moved along the wall. Each action was a necessary move in a slow game of chess that Evie intended to win. For every action, the man made a reaction. It wasn't until the stranger bumped into Jack's desk that Evie released a small smile.

In the blink of an eye, she had escaped and closed Jack's door behind her. She decided to take the back route out of the building, just in case. Evie figured that the new kid obviously wouldn't have any idea how much Evie knew about the building. She quickly opted for the private back entrance that was typically reserved to escort more high-profile people in and out of the premises without alerting the press. Of course, Evie had found it during one of her first trips to the department when she was still a little kid. That was also the day that she had accidentally locked herself in a supply closet until one of the janitors had stopped by for more toilet paper. Instead of deterring her, the entire interaction had only motivated her to map out the building. She still had the crayon layout of the building stuffed somewhere deep inside one of the miscellaneous files under her bed.

Evie glanced one more time over her shoulder and noticed that no one had followed her. She pushed against the door and headed out to attend to the next part of her questionable agenda.

Chapter 26

"Watch it, Lady!" A furious biker snarled as he zoomed over Evie's right foot. She stumbled back and watched as the man hurtled down the hill at a breakneck speed. His hair blew back in the strong wind as he swerved and mercilessly knocked into a corner vendor's sign.

A snicker escaped Evie's lips at the apparent instant Karma. Her foot pulsed in time to her heartbeat, but she was too far away from home to give up. She had just another block to go before she could finally sit down and enjoy the bumpy ride.

The boat ride was uneventful. Evie absently thanked the crew as she disembarked. Alcatraz stood within sight as Evie took in a deep gulp of ocean air. The abandoned prison looked like a scene from an ominous movie set just waiting for the director to scream action. She had the strangest feeling that there were people hiding just out of sight, prepared to jump into action at a moment's notice. She hesitantly glanced around the prison's recreational yard. Evie tilted her head up just enough so that she could see where the tops of the walls greeted the sky. It was no wonder that it was known as one of the world's most infamous prisons. Of course, Evie understood that what had partly made the prison so famous were the high-profile prisoners that had walked the halls. The place had been permanently shuttered in the early 1960s, but countless legends and ghost stories still lived on.

Evie walked across the massive area and settled against one of the large stairs that faced the rest of the yard. For a moment, she swore that she could hear the beginning of a yard fight, but then she looked around at all of the eager and bright-eyed tourists and realized that not for the first time, her imagination was getting the best of her.

A small little girl with pudgy cheeks and a missing front tooth hesitantly came up to Evie. Her eyes were lowered to the ground as she held out a small camera.

"Miss, do you mind taking a picture of me? It's my birthday."

The little voice sounded so quiet and high-pitched that it was momentarily hard to understand. Evie wasn't sure if the two things canceled each other out, but the tiny voice seemed to fill the massive expanse and get lost in a void all at the same time.

Evie rocked to her feet, "Sure. Do you want a picture facing the yard or the prison?"

"Both. It's my birthday so I might as well cover all of my bases."

The little girl looked up expectantly at Evie. Noticing her earlier mistake, Evie added, "Happy birthday. How old are you?"

The little girl stood on the tips of her toes as her green jumpsuit blew around her ankles. It looked comically similar to a bad prison outfit. Evie realized that the kid was likely trying to emulate prison garb.

"Seven. I'm basically middle-aged. You see, I have this theory that most people rarely age after seven. I mean everyone gets a bigger body after seven, but I mean in the head. Some people just stay seven."

"Wise words. You're a very sage person for only seven."

"Thank you," The little girl preened at the compliment and then gripped the sides of her jumpsuit as she gave a small half-bow.

"Here. Face the prison. Next we can take photos of you facing the yard. Does that sound like a plan?"

"Sounds like a plan."

The little girl clapped her hands together as if they had just finished an important business meeting and the weight of an entire company was precariously placed on her small bird-like shoulders.

Evie dutifully snapped several photos and changed the angles as the little girl instructed. She took two more photos before a panicked voice cut through the air, "Angelica!"

Instantly, the little girl's demeanor changed. She slumped her shoulders a little more and turned into a much younger version of the person that Evie has been speaking with. The less mature demeanor more closely aligned with the expected behavior of a child.

"I'm here, Mummy!"

A panicked woman in her late thirties rushed over. She donned straight khaki pants and a Hawaiian shirt that seemed only slightly geographically confused. For a moment, Evie discreetly glanced between mother and daughter. Their noses were similar and their eyes looked the same, but Evie suddenly understood the comment that the child had so astutely made.

"I'm so sorry! She just wanders off on tours. Thank you so much for watching her."

The woman placed a palm against the child's back and sighed in relief as if holding and touching the back of the makeshift prison outfit helped her to understand that Angelica was fine.

"She actually kept me entertained. It's not everyday that I get to meet a very distinguished birthday girl," Evie gently joked as she looked down at the child.

Angelica giggled as her mom's face visibly reddened. "We offered to take her to other places, but she refused. She insisted on visiting Alcatraz and seeing the history."

The woman placed air quotes around the last part, but Evie had no doubt in her mind that Angelica had been serious about wanting to see the history. The mother then continued, "I blame all of the gangster and prohibition documentaries available online. There is just too much knowledge accessible to people who are too young to understand."

"I understand more than you think, Mama." The little voice called from a few feet below as Angelica's gaze remained transfixed on the camera screen. Her tiny finger impatiently flicked through the new photos.

For a moment, Evie felt that she had a strong case for reincarnation. Angelica was much too mature for seven. In fact, her precocious nature threatened to make her older than her own mother. As the rays of sun hit down on the yard, it created a halo of light around Angelica's hair, Evie could swear that she had noticed several fine wrinkles and creases around the once cherubic child's face. The illusion quickly disappeared once Angelica stepped out of the reflecting light cast into the yard from one of the prison windows.

Impossible.

Evie shrugged, "It is a large part of the history of San Francisco. For better or for worse. It can't just disappear."

"I wish! This place is horrible. I could barely make it here just thinking about the poor innocent people that had been sent here under false pretenses. It still happens today, you know."

"What?"

"People are still put in prison for crimes that they didn't commit. The system is flawed. Here."

Angelica's mother reached into her purse and pulled out a bright yellow flier. An image of handcuffs and sad frowning emojis covered the paper. In the center, there was a time and a date that Evie couldn't exactly read.

"It's for tomorrow."

"That sounds interesting."

"Yes. Thank you for watching my Angelica. Angelica, say goodbye to the nice lady."

Angelica stood to the side of her mother. She looked up at Evie and sent her a coy smile. Her small baby voice was completely at odds with the bright light behind her devious eyes as she called, "Bye."

Chapter 27

Clouds hovered close to the sea and made it more difficult than usual for the captain to navigate. Seagulls flew around in the sky as they moved between the defunct prison and the mainland.

The boat back to the mainland was a welcomed break from all human interaction. Evie wondered if she had just forgotten the acute perceptiveness of children. Maybe Evie had lost her edge.

Droplets of ocean water landed on Evie's face as she unlocked her phone and scrolled through her photos. Her fingers stopped once she reached the image that she had so carefully taken of the paper on Jack's desk. Evie flexed her fingers and zoomed into the names.

She narrowed her eyes and glanced at the first name on the list. Evie wondered if each name correlated to the list of addresses on the right section of the page.

"Only one way to find out." Evie typed the first name into her phone and waited for the search to load. The service over the bumpy waves was spotty at best. Evie impatiently tapped her foot against the damp boat floor as the loading indicator in the center of her screen made slow and circular loops. A circular death spiral.

Finally, the page loaded and revealed several links, but none of them seemed relevant. Not one of the links spoke about a person named Rose MKenna. One link mentioned a professional named Rose that lived in Texas, but that felt like more than a stretch.

Unconvinced, Evie flitted back to the image on her phone and then typed in the address on the opposite side of the paper. The spinning loading wheel once again began another round of merciless circling.

Evie groaned as she looked up at the sky and noticed that the clouds were slowly turning gray. It was a sure sign that it was likely to rain. A mental note that only added to Evie's impatience.

Eventually, the search results appeared with several promising links. Evie scrolled down the first page of results and felt a jolt of surprise trail down her spine.

Apparently, the name wasn't about a person, but a massive company. The company named Rose MKenna seemed to have deep roots within the city of San Francisco. Some of the press from the last five years was less than flattering.

Evie methodically searched names and locations from the scrap of paper and received the same results. Each name belonged to a company that was located somewhere within California. All of the company names sounded like women's names and Evie had a sneaking suspicion that they all belonged to the same parent company.

However, the answers only left Evie with more questions. Why was Jack researching such an odd list of companies? On paper, none of them seemed suspicious. They ranged from niche perfume selections to modern furniture stores. Although the companies had less than squeaky reputations in terms of the environment, they all seemed legitimate.

"Let's find out if they're as real as they look," Evie muttered as she absently rubbed her hands over her arms. She tried to create enough friction so that the action could warm her frozen limbs. Instead of waiting inside of the warm cabin of the boat, Evie had opted to stand outside on the frigid deck. She wanted to avoid the prying eyes of curious tourists.

Paranoia was something that weaved its way into Evie's everyday life and she had no intention of changing direction just because her fingers felt a little prickly. Luckily, the boat engines had slowed and Evie knew that it was almost time to disembark.

Without thinking, Evie typed in the address of the perfume store and decided to follow the directions. Out of all of the stores, it felt like the most possible bet for a fake front. Why would anyone ever spend such copious amounts of money on a perfume? She had a few guesses, but decided to put them to bed until there was more evidence.

Evie couldn't imagine how a niche and relatively unknown perfumery could survive in San Francisco. How could any semi-successful company afford to pay thousands of dollars each month just for rent?

Maybe Uncle Jack had stumbled onto something similar to what the missing woman had found. Maybe that's why she had disappeared. Evie nibbled on her lower lip as she headed to the front of the boat. She had beat the rest of the wandering tourists and quickly stepped down the slanted plank with ease. She stomped up the slick metal steps and stood back on the wooden dock.

Once on solid ground, she glanced down at her phone and realized that she wouldn't have to wait long for answers. It appeared that the perfume store was only around the corner from the next block of tiny stores.

Evie nodded her head and then prepared to find out the truth. She increased her speed as excitement filled her previously frozen bones. Her cheeks flushed with warmth as she dipped and dodged between loud tourists. She noticed that although it was only the afternoon, many people had already headed back inside due to the unfavorable weather. The knowledge only elevated Evie's mood as she enjoyed the freedom of a wider street.

Chapter 28

Women entered and exited the store on a fragrant revolving basis. Each lady walked in empty-handed and strolled out with a small pink paper bag that looked crafted from the finest material. Surely, the place was new. However, the sheer number of people that entered the store hinted at a much longer history. It typically took years to establish such a loyal clientele.

Curiosity got the better of Evie as she self-consciously wiped her sweaty palms against the sides of her pants. She ran her fingers through her dull hair like a makeshift brush. Evie knew that her hair lacked the luster showcased by many of the ladies that buzzed around the store. She understood that her clothes weren't exactly that trendy wealthy neutral color. Evie hoped that the details wouldn't make her stand out. Decided, she swung open the old-fashioned door as a multitude of fragrances immediately greeted her senses.

The room looked clean and sophisticated in a way that only wealthy stores could afford to so effortlessly execute. A perfectly crafted combination of elegance and opulence. The windows above the cash register were stained glass and depicted a view of the Golden Gate bridge on a sunny day.

A woman in a long flowy black dress and an engraved nameplate promptly approached Evie. She did one cursory glance over Evie's appearance and visibly stiffened. However, the bright practiced smile never left the saleswoman's lips.

"Hi, how can I help you? My name is Kevin, but everyone calls me Ken."

Evie didn't respond right away as she gave the entire store a slow glance. Her eyes then trailed over the nameplate before she replied, "Hi, Ken. I'm just looking for a new perfume. My friend mentioned this shop and I decided to give it a try."

Ken's eyes narrowed as her smile slanted at the corners with displeasure. Several other women entered the store. They all donned designer bags and freshly painted nails. Silent symbols of a club that Evie had always observed from the outside.

Unwilling to be deterred, Evie arched an eyebrow and waited for Ken to respond. Ken nibbled her lower lip in a fashion that closely resembled a hamster chewing on the edges of its water bottle.

"Yes, we offer the finest hand-crafted fragrances in all of San Francisco. However, the price point can be a bit steep. There is a corner drugstore just at the end of the block that also offers scents at a more attainable price point."

For a minute, Evie considered shooting the woman. However, the intricate glass bottles didn't deserve such abuse if Ken's body crushed them in her fall. Instead, Evie sighed and decided that it wasn't worth the bullet.

She regarded the other woman with a cool smile, "That's very thoughtful of you. I appreciate your suggestion, but the drugstore is likely more your style. I'm here because this store offers something that I want."

Evie kept her smile in place and quickly sidestepped the attendant. The crowd quickly swallowed her whole and offered her some protection from the unpleasant interaction.

Curious, Evie picked up a sample bottle and felt the weight of the glass. Thin gold letters called the fragrance, Sunshine. The list of ingredients seemed normal enough and the particular notes were exotic, but still complimentary. Evie spritzed a bit onto a sample stick and tentatively inhaled. The scent of peonies instantly reached Evie's sensitive nose as she started to sneeze.

A few customers looked over, but then quickly returned back to their potential purchases. Evie glanced around and noticed a small backroom just to the right of the cash register. The placement of the hidden room felt odd given that the checkout section had been placed near a window. Evie was willing to bet that the slim area led to a well-hidden back room that was smartly disguised as storage for additional products. If so, it was likely that the more unsavory business took place behind the curtains only a few steps away from the unsuspecting crowd.

The wide selection of perfume was nearly overwhelming. A sign to the right described darker scents with stronger base notes. Intrigued, Evie walked over and realized that most of the scents in the designated area were stereotypically more masculine than Evie had expected. Many smelt of cigars or grass and in some way the scents appealed to Evie's preferences. Now, Evie finally realized why the concept of purchasing perfume had always eluded her. Most perfumes that she had tried included specific floral scents that irritated her allergies. The reality of breaking out into hives never seemed like a worthwhile side effect. Now, the scents on the table caused no such reaction and Evie took in a greedy breath as her lungs filled with relief.

A sudden presence pushed into Evie's awareness. She discreetly turned to the left and found people completely immersed in their own lives. To the right, Evie noticed that the worker from earlier was following Evie's movements like a hawk.

Feeling petty, Evie decided to purchase one of the bottles. She gazed at the price tag and nearly flinched at the additional zeros, but decided that she still had a little money left over in her savings. After all, Evie rarely spent money outside of the occasional dumpster dive diner. She took her time and settled on a medium sized bottle with a bolder scent.

Satisfied, Evie walked over to the cash register. A young brunette practically cheered, "Yay! That's an excellent choice. Not many people tend to pick it out, but it's definitely one of our more original options."

The cashier kindly rang Evie up and then wrapped the perfume box inside of bright pink floral paper. The cashier gingerly placed the perfume inside of one of the nicely constructed paper bags that Evie had noticed earlier in her impulsive shopping spree.

As a finishing touch, the woman behind the counter even placed two pieces of white tissue paper inside of the bag. It looked like a perfectly wrapped gift. The kind of gift that was nearly too expensive to open.

When Evie was a kid, she had often struggled to open presents that were too nicely wrapped. She had worried that the beautiful packaging would always end up being better than the hidden gift. Her father had always pushed her to open the presents while her mom had always encouraged her to wait for the right moment. But what if the right moment never came? What if Evie waited and waited until she finally opened the gift and the box of chocolates had turned hard and spoiled? But then again, there was always the possibility of opening a gift and ending up with bargain socks that had been tactfully disguised behind a wall of promising wrapping paper and a shiny red bow.

If Evie didn't know any better, she would have assumed that people were purchasing an experience more so than actual perfume. The show did little to impress Evie, but she enjoyed the idea of having a reusable bag for her next gift.

She paid and made a show of holding the bag high as she walked out of the store. Evie's gaze locked with Ken's as she exited. Ken's cheeks flushed with embarrassment as she turned away and headed into the back room.

It was an oddly childish victory but for the moment, Evie had no intention of discounting even the smallest win. The biggest battle still managed to elude her. The knowledge that something crept just out of reach threatened to drive her mad. A dark shadow followed behind Evie even though there wasn't a cloud in the sky.

Chapter 29

Evie tentatively pulled out the white tissue paper. It felt heavy and plush between her fingers. She skimmed over the contents until her eyes noticed a circular emblem inscribed on the bottom of the bag. It looked similar to a massive cursive letter D with an infinity sign looped around the outer corners. As far as branding, Evie had never seen the logo, but then again she rarely attended boutique San Francisco perfumeries.

"Maybe it will be more promising at night." Evie pulled at the sleeve of her top and rolled a loose string between her fingers. She figured that she had a few hours to kill and decided to head back home before the main event.

Chapter 30

The newspaper stand near home looked oddly quiet as Evie headed inside. Her eyes narrowed at the same stranger that had dutifully manned the shop for several shifts too long. Evie grabbed a lighter near the top of the counter and handed it over along with one of the useless magazines. Her fingers selected the item before her eyes bothered to look at the cover.

"Are you a regular?" The man behind the counter rang up the two items and held out his hand to accept payment.

Relieved at such an easy start to the conversation, Evie tentatively nodded her head. Realizing she was missing an opportunity, Evie cleared her throat, "Yes. What happened to the man that usually works here?"

"He won a cruise trip for his family. I live two doors down from him. I agreed to help at the shop for a little bit of cash while I'm working on getting a new job. Lucky, bastard."

Evie had to agree that it seemed like a great stroke of luck. Especially, for someone that worked so hard for so many years on end. It felt like justice, but the idea of a properly balanced universe didn't seem plausible. It seemed like the entire system was always rigged in someone else's favor. Evie nodded her head and tried to feel happy for her friend. The answer seemed plausible enough at face value, but Evie knew better than to just accept things at first glance.

"That's good. He deserves something nice."

"Don't we all?" The man tossed both useless purchases into a black plastic bag and handed them over to Evie.

"Thanks."

Evie stepped back onto the sidewalk and mumbled, "So much for a strong lead."

Saturday
November 2, 2019
11:50pm

Chapter 31

The street lights cast a faint glow against the sides of the buildings as Evie once again returned to the scene of the unsolved murder. She unscrewed her water bottle and sighed as the taste of cheap vodka slid down her throat. It was bottom tier stuff, but it wasn't like Evie was about to complain. It did the job. A wave of heat swirled down her throat and landed in her belly just as her gaze locked with the top of Coit Tower.

After leaving the convenience store, Evie had spent the majority of her time scampering around town. Her aimless pursuit had brought her into a liquor store where she had purchased the second to the cheapest bottle of vodka. Evie had crouched behind an out-of-service city bus and poured out the water to make room for the vodka. A little kid had spotted her crouched position from across the street, but one irritated glare had set the youngster straight. There was no need for every nosey kid in San Francisco to know her business. Usually, Evie tried to be at least patient with kids, but it wasn't every day that a kid had unknowingly caught her at a low point.

Scram.

The word was equally as effective when physically portrayed on the lean features of her face. The kid reacted as if Evie had screamed her sentiments. In the blink of an eye, the child had quickly scampered away to catch up to its mother.

Maybe Evie was dancing closer to the edge of the knife and just waiting for the right moment to fall off. She felt close to unhinged and more than likely drunk as she kept walking.

Impossible.

Evie told herself that she enjoyed drinking to take the edge off and lately life just seemed a little sharper than usual. A few more drinks during the day seemed only logical.

Slowly, Evie returned to reality. The lights from the city caressed the bottom of the white tower like the hand of an adoring lover. A slow shudder wracked Evie's form as liquid melancholy swept through her bones.

The streets seemed quiet. The last visitors had long since returned back to their hotel rooms. Tucked safely inside of their queen beds and away from all the darker truths lurking in the less than tourist-friendly corners of the night. Evie loved every inch of that darkness which told the truth about her home. There was no such thing as a squeaky clean picture. Some painters were just more skilled at hiding the mess. An image of a Monet painting popped into Evie's mind as she skulked around in the darkness. Each brushstroke was a supposed disaster that eventually combined with others to make an unrivaled masterpiece.

From her front pocket, Evie pulled out her lock picking kit. The case was well worn and Evie hoped that the tower was still a few years behind in security. The last thing that Evie wanted to do was set off a silent alarm when Jack was on duty. She unscrewed the cap of her bottle and took a generous swig. The liquid tasted closer to water as Evie's senses continued to dull while her anxiety drifted into the bay.

Evie's fingers worked on autopilot. She infrequently swiveled her head to check for potential onlookers. Unsurprisingly, she couldn't see a damn thing past the bushes.

A soft *click* interrupted the quiet. The corners of Evie's lips curled up into a smile as she opened the window and crept inside. It wasn't exactly elegant as she toppled several feet down and landed on the unforgiving floor. Evie mouthed a silent curse as she gripped her head and glowered at the window that she had practically pried open. It wasn't her best attempt at breaking and entering.

Blindly, Evie picked up her bottle and then retrieved the pieces of her lock picking set which were sprawled around the floor. She turned on her phone flashlight and tried to get a sense of exactly where in the tower she had landed.

Blurry faces and busy hands greeted Evie's line of sight. Instinctively, Evie put her hands up and waited to get arrested. *Wait until Uncle Jack hears about this.*

Chapter 32

Evie felt her heart as it threatened to pound out of her chest. The scent of her own fear tainted the air and burned Evie's nose. She kept absolutely still as she waited for the people around her to make the first move. Evie waited and then waited some more.

Eventually, Evie pried open her eyes and glanced around the room. Her heart rate slowly returned to normal.

"Idiot."

Evie groaned as she glanced around the room and noticed the intricate murals. She couldn't believe how stupid she was being. Her lips wrapped around the top of the bottle as she took a small sip to center her jittery nerves. The murals were definitely not going to arrest her. Not even the painted cops would tell on her.

Satisfied, Evie shoved her tools into her front pocket and then patted the handgun neatly tucked into the back of her pants. The cold handle reminded Evie that she was still very much alive.

An odd noise caught Evie's attention. She held her breath and tried to listen for it again. Evie had sworn that the guards rarely entered the tower during nightly patrols. Maybe she was running on outdated information.

Her feet took her to the stairs which led up to the top of Coit Tower. Evie strained her ears to hear even the faintest of sounds. She had a difficult time discerning where the commotion was coming from. The faint city noises seemed to echo into the room from the opened window.

A weak sound came from some distance away. Evie felt inclined to think that the growing commotion was just the noises from down the hill. However, her gut said that it was headed in her direction. Eventually, the distant footsteps grew louder as they approached at an unhurried pace. Evie nibbled on her lower lip and desperately crept up the stairs. The tiny phone flashlight and her alcohol-laden body refused to cooperate. Desperate, Evie ascended the stairs on all fours. She desperately hugged the wall for support. Evie felt like an infant crawling to the top of the stairs.

"Not getting caught. Not today. Definitely not getting caught climbing up some stairs like a baby," Evie's knees pounded into the corner of each stair as if the action could help lock her in place. Her palms scrambled against the steps and landed in something sticky. Evie pulled away her fingers with such force that her body creaked back and threatened to tumble down the spiral stairs.

"Nope. Nope."

Evie tossed herself forward and her face smashed into the corner of one of the unforgiving steps. Relieved, Evie continued to climb as her face ached from the rough smack. She lost track of time as her body ascended without question. Evie could no longer hear the impending footsteps over the sound of her own heavy breathing and she no longer cared to check if anyone was behind her. No reasonable night shift guard would bother walking all the way up to the top of the tower. At least, not for minimum wage.

Evie held her breath as she stuck out her hand and felt the frigid door to the roof beneath her palm. The final barrier.

"Shit."

For a moment, Evie's hand traveled to the back of her waistband. She then rolled her eyes at the momentary stupidity. Why would she even consider firing a gun at a locked door? That was definitely on the list of best ways to have a security guard call for backup.

Her fingers dug around within her front pocket and retrieved the lock picking tools. The light next to the door appeared broken. Usually, armed doors in public settings flickered a slight inconsistent red to indicate that they were armed.

"I must be lucky." Evie patiently waited for the smallest click before she pressed her shoulder against the door and shoved. A low whine echoed around the room as the heavy door groaned in protest of opening a few inches. The hairs on the back of Evie's neck rose and her body tensed in anticipation. She was sure that at any second, a stern voice would call out from the darkness and becken her back down the stairs. Any moment now, a disembodied voice would shout out and entreat her to leave the tower.

Jack would never let her live this down. She drew in a deep fractured gasp and waited for what felt like an eternity. The silence stretched on and Evie wiggled around the barely open door. Her thighs scraped against the doorframe as her arms kept the actual door firmly restrained. She needed to avoid creating any additional noises. It was a miracle the guard hadn't noticed the first time. The doorframe bit into the skin of Evie's thighs and hips, but eventually she was able to shimmy to the rooftop.

City lights flickered like lightning bugs on a hot summer's night. There had to be at least one light turned on for every soul in the city. Evie glanced in the direction of the bay and noticed with bleak fascination how the darkness temporarily devoured the light until it was once again beat back from the shore.

"I've waited a long time for this."

Chapter 33

A tall slim outline embraced the darkness like a spectral figure. It seemed content to sneak around and feed off the living. The figure's shoulders were slumped at an awkward angle and gave the impression of a distinctly broken neck.

Evie stood her ground as a strange sense of calm swept over her body. An odd whisper in the back of her mind spoke in a language about a degree away from comprehension. However, the feeling in her gut remained clear. Evie had always felt that she'd meet the instigator of death in San Francisco. She just never thought that he'd look so unassuming.

"Do you remember me? I definitely thought of you over the years. Dreamt of this moment. I must admit that even in my worst dreams, you appeared more horrified. I'm a little disappointed, but that's something that we can fix."

Each word was punctuated by the hidden figure taking a measured step out of the darkness. Slow, unhurried, and obviously jovial steps. It was as if the mere action of walking closer to Evie had to be savored and properly executed.

Evie knew who it was after the third step. She would recognize that face anywhere. Her face scrunched in confusion as she tried to understand why the god of death would look like the man that she had sent to prison. Danvers had made her job easy by taking his own life. She didn't feel guilty. Not at all.

After a second thought, Evie squared her shoulders. She was sure that Danvers had somehow faked his own death. Logic compelled Evie to observe the facts and to perceive the scene in front of her eyes without the fog of liquor taking charge. The momentary shock had managed to jumpstart her senses. Bias whispered in the back of her mind that the god of death would never come to her in the form of a man that she didn't regret sending to jail. All of the evidence had pointed in his direction. But still.

A strange niggling that had itched around the corners of Evie's mind when she had first worked on the case came back with a vengeance. The man that she had sent to jail didn't have the typical persona of a serial killer. He had appeared like an odd ship out to see. Drowning in the legal waters as if he hadn't freely sailed into trouble in the first place. It was pretty easy to avoid committing multiple murders.

It had always surprised Evie when Danvers had appeared so shocked at the accusation. His hunted face was permanently etched into Evie's memory. How he had cautiously peered around every corner as she had led him to the interrogation room, directed him to a holding cell, and even testified against him in court.

However, something in Danver's eyes had hinted at an inexplicable fear. Perhaps, a motivation just out of grasp. Or, the entire time that Evie had spent observing the man had been a moment carefully constructed to deceive her. Maybe Danvers just wanted to play her emotions like a violin.

Now, Arthur appeared taller as an ominous aura emanated from his body in waves. He looked nearly giddy as his dark eyes greedily drank in the sight of Evie. It was as if he could hardly believe that she was at the top of the tower.

"I put you away for life, Danvers."

Evie cut into the silence with a simple leading statement. She didn't really know what else to say to a man that had faked his own death, escaped from prison, and clearly taken his time planning to get his revenge.

A twisted smile pulled at the corners of the man's mouth. His dark eyes gleamed as he took a single step closer and crossed the barrier of light created by flickering lamps. Half of the motion activated flood lamps had died out a long time ago. One portion of the roof remained permanently shrouded in darkness while the other was sporadically illuminated in a faint glow before being shoved into momentary nothingness. The snatches of visibility left Evie feeling off-kilter as she closely watched Arthur's every move.

A deep chuckle escaped from the back of his throat, "I'm not Arthur."

Chapter 34

Silence engulfed the rooftop as Evie struggled to understand what Arthur was saying. Maybe he had changed his name after faking his death and escaping prison. It seemed plausible.

She contemplated reaching for the hidden gun, but faltered. Evie needed to know more. Curiosity beat out self-preservation. Evie asked, "What do you call yourself?"

Realistically, Evie knew that she needed to stall in order to give herself time to come up with a plan. She also needed to drag out the conversation to have even the slightest chance at being discovered by the night shift security. Now, the security that she had so desperately hidden from had become her best chance at rescue.

Evie hadn't told a single soul where she was headed before she had left her cozy apartment. Her best bet was to stall. The second option was to take matters into her own hands. However, the idea of taking a life threw her off balance.

Questions spun around in the back of Evie's mind like a furious tornado. Would she have time to reach for the gun? Did she have the courage to pull the trigger? Did she want to pull the trigger? Was this her way out?

A piece of Evie felt disconnected from the moment. Floating. Her eyes remained locked on Arthur's tall frame. Arthur appeared larger than she had remembered. His shoulders were more filled out and his demeanor had shifted from a meek nervous lamb to a wolf eager for the kill.

He was finally the man that Evie had imagined in her nightmares. The version that had haunted her dreams for months. When she had been on the case, it had felt like she had always just missed him. Evie had always gotten the sense that the killer enjoyed playing a sick game of cat and mouse. A game that Evie had no intention of playing, but had gotten cowed into nonetheless. It had almost felt like the murderer had been trying to trick her. But the joke was on Arthur, Evie had found him.

The man's gaze hardened to steel as a haughty air of superiority oozed from his skin, "You locked up my twin, Arthur. In case you couldn't guess, we're identical twins."

Liar. Evie narrowed her eyes in disbelief. There was no record of a second child. Arthur clearly was more deranged than Evie had originally thought and that was saying something. Evie held her ground as she bit her lower lip in disapproval.

Of course, Arthur noticed the distrust clearly written across Evie's delicate features. He continued, "I don't believe that my parents were fond of my choices growing up. They disowned me when I started to get into trouble at school. A few greased palms later and all official records of me were wiped from existence. They gave me more than enough funds to disappear, but they still wanted nothing to do with me. It's ironic if you really think about it. My parents gave me the gift of anonymity when they pulled me from the records and officially disowned me. Little did they know just how helpful that would be in getting away with murder. Literally. Everything ended up being pinned on Arthur. He had tried to convince you that he was innocent, but you were just too stuck to see the truth. Arthur was weak. He lacked the conviction to even murder a rabid dog, let alone an innocent woman. No, such strong urges are born into you. The need to destroy and thrive in that destruction is an addiction. Some would even say a calling."

The man that had adamantly declared that he wasn't Arthur brandished a small knife out of the back pocket of his jeans. The sparse light flickered against the metal blade.

Evie didn't know if she could believe him, but she decided to ask, "What's your name?"

"My name is Ian Danvers. My soft idiot brother took the fall for my crimes because you were too incompetent to find me."

"You just said that all evidence of you was scrubbed from the record," Evie testily replied. It wasn't the best idea to argue with a known serial killer, but he had touched on a nerve. Evie had never truly felt like she deserved the role of private detective. She had loved putting pieces together that other people had missed or actively ignored. Solving a case usually felt like putting together a puzzle without clear instructions or all of the pieces. It really tested a person's wit.

As an outsider looking in, it was easier to notice all of the details that people willfully ignored. Individuals often turned away from the truth to protect their personal level of comfort. If Ian really wasn't Arthur, then Evie had failed to see the bigger picture.

Evie's searching eyes took a cursory glance around the rooftop as she calculated possible escape routes. Unfortunately, Ian Danvers blocked the main exits. The elevator and stairs were firmly out of bounds thanks to a tall muscular psychopath intent on either killing or severely maiming her. Neither option sounded particularly appealing.

Ian's face grew cold. A muscle on the side of his jaw clenched at Evie's words. He fiddled around with the knife. His long sure fingers bobbed and weaved away from the blade as his tongue spewed out a quick reproach.

"Well, my brother was innocent. He ended up taking the blame. I always knew he was soft. Too soft for prison and too useless to thrive in this world. The world is full of efficient hunters and useless prey. It's extremely rare to have the honor of hunting big game."

Ian's words churned the bile within Evie's stomach. She knew exactly what he was implying as his eyes trailed over her skin.

To center her mind, Evie dedicated part of her attention to watching the knife as it aimlessly weaved between Ian's fingers. The action reminded Evie of a bored student twirling a pencil during a particularly annoying lecture. The realization that Ian was likely just as familiar around a knife as a student with a pencil made her skin crawl.

His deranged skillset grew more obvious with every second that they spent together. It became more and more apparent that Evie had little chance of escaping unless she kept Ian mentally engaged. It appeared that Evie didn't have the luxury of boring him. Luckily, she had enough questions to ensure that her curiosity felt genuine.

Evie knew that she was walking a fine line as she asked, "Why didn't you intervene? The case had dragged on for months. Two of the jurors had been on the fence about your brother. Deliberations alone had lasted weeks. Even after Arthur had been convicted, there was never a letter or an anonymous tip. No clue or hint pointed away from his direction. The night of the final murder, Arthur had said that he had been in the building waiting to meet a friend. Conveniently, the friend had never shown up. He had no one to corroborate his story and easily lacked an alibi."

Evie suddenly put the case together. The real answer hit her square between her eyes with the force of the bullet. She shook her head in confusion as Ian simply chuckled, "Putting it together? Maybe you're not as dumb as you look. You know, you're actually pretty attractive when you're sleeping."

The final shoe dropped. Ian was the one who had been snooping around her apartment recently. He had managed to infiltrate her life without raising a single alarm. The thought of having a crazed lunatic slinking around her apartment on the nights where she had been incapacitated twisted her belly. What else had Ian done while she was drunk and supposedly safely nestled into her studio for the night?

"You were in my room when I was asleep? Did you do anything?"

The real unsaid question rang through the chilled air. Waiting.

"Don't worry, Evie. I'm just a killer."

Ian tossed his hands up in mock innocence, but his tone rang true. Apparently, he abided to some warped moral code that Evie had little interest in picking apart at the moment.

Ian sighed, "Keep going, Evie. I want to hear what you've pieced together and then I'll let you know if you've got it right."

A sick smile crossed Ian's face as he turned into the cat who ate the canary. He drawled, "Actually, let's make it a game. You guess and I'll tell you if you're right. If you're right then you can take a step away. If you're wrong then I get to take a step closer. If you reach the edge of the railing before I reach you then you'll be safe for the night. If I manage to get to you first then I will have my revenge. It will be fun."

"You really like games."

Ian shrugged, "I suppose that I never really grew up. Some tasks require a certain level of child-like wonder."

He's insane. The thought unnerved Evie in a way that she struggled to put into words.

The heavy silence weighed against Evie's shoulders as she pondered her next move. How could she be expected to trust anything that Ian said? What were the odds that he would actually tell the truth even if Evie guessed correctly? The game was rigged in his favor. There was very little room for error on Evie's part. She hoped that agreeing to play would at least buy her a little time. From her stakeout around the tower, she knew that the guards usually changed shifts at two in the morning. It surely had already passed one. What happened? Where were the guards?

A sudden understanding crept down Evie's spine. Tonight was daylight savings.

Evie had to stay alive for an extra hour as the clock turned back. Damn daylight savings. Of all the days that the clock would be set back an hour, it had to be when she was stuck on a roof with a crazed murderer. She sucked in a shaky breath and clasped her shaking hands together. Evie just needed to stall for the most important 60 minutes of her life.

Sunday
November 3rd of 2019
1:00am

Chapter 35

One more hour. Evie decided to play Ian's game. Not that she had much of a choice if she wanted to get any information. She bitterly pointed out, "You could lie. Even if I'm right, what's to stop you from saying I guessed wrong?" Evie folded her arms over her chest.

Ian released a belly-shaking chuckle, "Nothing, that's what makes this game so exciting. You should know better than to trust a murderer, Evie. Of course, it's not like you're in a position to go with another choice. This is the only choice. Well, the other choice is death, but I hope you don't pick that option so soon. That would really ruin our fun."

He bounced from one foot to the other. The excited energy unsettled Evie. She struggled to stay calm as her feet remained firmly rooted in place.

For a man in his mid-thirties, Ian at times tended to behave much younger. Like an excited vicious kid, eager to escape his timeout and terrorize the small bugs in the backyard. Oddly cruel.

"Fine," Evie ground out from between her teeth.

"Perfect, now what were you saying about me not sending letters to Arthur when he was in jail?"

"You never sent anything to indicate that Arthur was innocent. Not one letter or clue to the court. Not even one attempt at intimidation of a jury member. No evidence tampering. Nothing."

Before Evie could continue, Ian groaned, "These are facts. You will never move to the door by just telling me simple facts. What is your reasoning? The logic? What about connecting the dots or do they no longer teach you that skill? How can you solve a case if you aren't trying to see how the pieces fit?"

Ian was taunting her as he rocked on the very back of his heels with obvious excitement. He enjoyed seeing her squirm.

Evie decided to start small. "You strike me as a man that enjoys getting what he wants. What was the point of going out on a limb?"

Evie knew that Ian could lie and easily ruin the so-called game. She didn't have much of a choice.

Ian rolled his eyes. "Wow, if this is what you're going to give me then we might as well stop playing and I can just kill you now."

He took a step closer as his dark eyes flickered in irritation. Evie quickly lifted up her hands and shouted, "Fine! You never sent anything to help free Arthur because you wanted him to stay in jail. You wanted him to take the fall because if he died no one would look for you! He was your scapegoat, but he was also your brother."

A pleased smile stretched along Ian's face, "That's right. Take a step closer to safety."

**Sunday
November 3, 2019
1:45 am**

Chapter 36

Evie nodded her head and took one large step. She needed to get out of here before Ian grew bored or irritated. He was unstable and emotional in a high-intensity situation and that made him dangerous. He was definitely not going to make this simple, but since when did Evie ever get anything handed to her? That ease and luck had left her years ago.

"Keep going."

"You didn't want Arthur getting out of jail. He was the bow designed to wrap-up your previous murders. The perfect answer to your problem because you knew that he would never tell on you. Arthur was more afraid of you than he was of going to jail."

Ian gave a slow nod of approval and called, "Take another step closer to the door."

She took a generous single stride and waited. Evie tried to guess how many more observations she would need to make before she would be able to reach the railing. Her gaze traveled back to the floor as she craned her neck and desperately tried to mentally divide the remaining distance. She estimated that it would take about three or four more wide steps to supposedly reach safety. Of course, that was assuming that all of her future guesses were flawless.

Ian stretched his arms and reached up to the inky black sky as if he had just run a marathon. The promise of bloodshed thrilled Ian. He seemed to love watching Evie squirm.

"Apparently, you perfectly understand why Arthur decided to stay inside of prison. Why do you think that he killed himself?"

Evie momentarily widened her eyes. She was about to answer, but stopped as she took note of the satisfied look lurking behind Ian's gaze. He appeared so sure of himself. The certainty in his posture caused Evie to throw her previous theory out of the window. Instead, she answered, "That doesn't bother you. Why Arthur killed himself isn't really the major concern."

"Very true. What is the major concern?"

Ian's face grew intent as if he was waiting to hear every single one of Evie's words. It was a bit of a trap. He wanted Evie to fail. In fact, he wasn't expecting Evie to succeed, at all. The first step was a freebie and the second was unexpected. Now, this question was designed to see Evie lose.

She shifted her weight from one foot to the other. Evie mentally reviewed every detail about the case. She pondered all of the information that she had gathered about past victims.

The photos from previous crime scenes flitted behind Evie's closed lids like a bad movie. She was powerless to escape the magnitude of such haunted images. Women drowned and burned beyond recognition. Maybe Evie really was looking at the devil.

Ian fit the profile of the killer like the perfect missing piece of the puzzle. Arthur's demeanor had never really fit. Evie saw it now. She noticed Ian's dark behavior and recognized his ability to take pleasure in Evie's distress. Ian ticked every box. His dangerous gaze remained expertly trained on her every move like a hound eager for the hunt. He was more beast than man. He had somehow managed to prowl around the city undetected for years.

Specific memories slowly stepped to the front of Evie's consciousness. She recalled how the profile of the murderer had hinted at an ego and an odd sense of self-importance. In addition, the final page of the official police report had described an individual that enjoyed functioning within a strict set of personally created rules. A person that couldn't stand to be wrong. According to the report, he craved his own personal brand of order.

One of Ian's victims had managed to escape and even testified at the trial. The woman had said that she'd never forget his evil face. A face that Evie now wondered if two people had shared. The survivor had said that the man that had tried to kill her couldn't stand being outsmarted by a woman. He had tried to chase her down through the woods. Luckily, the woman had managed to locate a group of campers that had taken her into their fold and helped her to get to safety.

"This isn't about your brother."

Evie knew that such a bold statement ran the risk of upsetting Ian and potentially throwing him into a rage. She treaded carefully and continued, "You let him rot in jail. What really upsets you is that I put him away. You're upset that I had managed to get so close to you in the first place. You had thought that you were so careful. But you were wrong. I had collected enough evidence to put you away for good. The only problem with identical twins is that the DNA is overwhelmingly similar. Because we didn't know that you existed, the entire case easily landed on Arthur. You were sloppy and then needed Arthur to pay the price for your mistakes. You don't want to avenge Arthur. You want to take revenge on me for yourself. It hurts your pride to know that a woman nearly had the best of you. It eats you from the inside, doesn't it?"

Evie sneered out the biting rhetorical question. Her teeth were bared as the last word hissed out from behind her locked jaw.

A vein pulsed on the side of Ian's forehead as his jaw remained tightly shut. Evie was sure that she was about to witness him snapping his teeth in half due to the pressure. His shoulders shook in obvious rage and small driblets of blood fell to the ground as Ian tightened his grip around the blade of the knife.

Evie gulped, but held her ground as she waited for Ian to answer. She wanted to keep him off-kilter so that it was easier for her to manipulate him. Her mind had been working in overdrive as she had carefully played Ian's twisted game. Evie knew that taking the long winding stairs was out of the question. Ian was too close and could easily grab her even if she twisted around him. The roof was too small for such a tactic. Evie had contemplated jumping from the tower, but the fall would surely kill her. However, what did Ian have in mind before deciding to grant her a chance at a quick eternal slumber? Likely, he planned to draw it out. Would jumping be easier? Was she fast enough to retrieve the gun and remove the safety? The same sense of heavy futility threatened to suffocate Evie as it landed on her shoulders like an invisible blanket. She thought through every option. Finally, Evie knew what she needed to do. For once, Evie felt at peace with her decision.

Her face remained passive as Ian continued to balk and bluster at her previous remark. The darkness remained heavy and the lights from the city appeared distant. It was as if the lights were actively trying to run away from the vast nothingness that surrounded them.

"Take one step closer to your freedom, Little Pest." A sharp edge laced into Ian's tone as he kept his gaze locked with Evie.

He added, "You're right."

Ian sliced through the air with the blade of the knife. He nodded, obviously impressed with Evie's understanding of the situation and continued, "How did you manage to circle so close to the truth after less than a year on the case? The idiots from the force had poked and prodded for years without even the slightest clue as to what they were doing. If it weren't for you, I would have already fully adjusted to my career change."

"Murdering women isn't a career path. It just makes you a psychopath."

Damn it. The words flew past Evie's lips without so much as a moment of hesitation. She knew that it wasn't likely that Ian was going to let her live. Even if she played by his rules. Whenever men made the rules, women tended to lose, even when they played perfectly. There wasn't much point in playing a game designed to see you lose. Still, Evie held her spot that was a little more than two long strides away from promised safety. The designated safe zone remained just a few feet away and part of Evie dreaded the idea of reaching it too soon. The consequences had the potential to be just the same as if she had lost.

A low chuckle drew Evie out of her thoughts. Ian clucked his tongue in disapproval, "You might have all of this figured out, but what do you know about the part that truly concerns you?"

Chapter 37

The question hung in the air as Evie tried to understand what Ian was talking about. She was relatively sure that the entire point of his appearance was to extract his revenge.

"You want revenge."

The deadpanned statement did little to appease Ian. Instead, he petulantly groaned, "Yes, but no. No matter, I will explain. You were my favorite target to date. I watched you for weeks and realized that you have a relatively sad and lifeless routine that's filled with pouring small bottles of liquor into cheap diner coffees. You get paid to scour through other people's private lives, but you hate it. At first, I wasn't sure what to make of your sad work, but then I realized that you're bored. You had appeared so full of life when investigating my case because you had purpose. I had to figure out a way to attract your attention and get you alone. It took some time, but I finally found a way to copy that thrill."

"The story about the woman in the tower." Evie finally understood what Ian was talking about.

"Yes. I made it up and kept it as vague and difficult to understand as possible. It wasn't hard to have a few people show up at the right time with the wrong information. People are more than willing to do an odd task for a generous amount of money if it doesn't seem risky. Lucky for me, there are more than enough starving artists willing to take on an odd job."

Evie hissed, "You fund your lifestyle by selling drugs from the back of your perfume store. It was under your family name, but I'm willing to bet that you have full control."

Evie made the assumption and wondered why it had taken her so long to connect the dots. Ian had a thriving business with roots in every profitable niche imaginable.

She had been lured to the top of the roof by a shell of a man. A ghost that traveled aimlessly around the city, looking to antagonize the living. Apparently, he had found the perfect woman to haunt. After all, Evie already considered herself stuck between the living and the dead. The past and the present. It was about time that someone finally made her choose.

"I thought that you were a thorough detective. Unfortunately, you're missing a few key details that make me think otherwise. Why would I need to sell drugs from my very successful and legitimate business?"

"Because you have expensive taste and so do your victims. The women you killed had all shopped at your perfumery. They're all well-funded and high-society and no one could fully connect the dots between their murders because no one would suspect that the connection could be something as small as a bottle of perfume. You created a personal hunting ground and then turned it into a place for women to obtain drugs. You knew that it would deter any squealers. Selling drugs to these women would keep them from mentioning your shop to the police. You don't sell drugs for money. It's your own twisted version of an insurance policy."

Ian grinned from ear to ear as he chuckled, "Take another step, Evie. You learn quickly."

Chapter 38

Evie could sense that her time was running out. Soon, the game would end and there would be nothing left to stop Ian from approaching. At least, he was entertained in the moment and that gave Evie hope that help would arrive.

For the second time, Evie's fingers ever so gently grazed against the cool metal handle that was barely concealed behind the waistband of her pants. At that moment, Evie decided that one of them wasn't walking away. She had every intention of making sure that it was Ian. The justice system had failed once.

No.

Evie had failed once because Ian had tricked her into putting away his own flesh and blood. It infuriated Evie on a deep level to know that he had decided to toss away his family like a used napkin. Arthur had served no purpose after cleaning up the initial blood spill. A lamb to the slaughter.

It burned Evie's insides. She couldn't recall the last time that she had even hugged her parents. It felt like a distant dream to even remember what their faces looked like. Her remaining memories were all vague images where bits and pieces were incorrectly melded together with sharp edges sticking out at odd angles. What was left of Evie's parents wasn't a bright memory, but a glob of moments copied and pasted together in the wrong order. The car accident had jumbled her mind. The horrific moments spent screaming in a burning car were the ones that overrode the rest.

The crash had killed something light and vibrant in Evie's core. It was as if the universe had suddenly shoved her into a blender and poured out something that was technically still every bit her, but also not even remotely the same.

"Why?"

A darkness flickered in the back of Ian's gaze as he growled, "This game does not involve you asking the questions."

"You have fun watching me squirm. An honest answer will likely make me cringe. Your game continues whether I like it or not."

Evie shifted from one foot to the other. She felt extremely uncomfortable, but tried her best to conceal her growing anxiety.

"It's like you've always known me," Ian playfully cooed as he waved the knife in a careless fashion and pointed it at his heart.

He continued, "Arthur never had what it took to live freely. He always let me take and take from him. I think he was stupid enough to believe that one day I would see his behavior as love, but it was always just an opportunity for me to twist the knife deeper. My only regret is that I wasn't the one who was able to finish the poor bastard."

Evie gave a low hiss and instinctively took half a step back before she realized her mistake. Of course, it was too late, Ian had already tracked the small motion with laser-like focus.

"No stealing spaces. One more step without permission and the game ends. And Evie?"

"What?"

"You were right. Your reactions are priceless. Now, for the reveal. I had you trying to solve a murder that didn't exist. You were running around town just to end up dead in the same fashion as the woman that you had read about in the newspaper."

Evie wasn't ruffled by the threat of death. Instead, it rolled off her shoulders as she asked, "How did you get the stories printed in the paper?"

"Simple. I didn't. I only needed to make one copy. I placed the stories in the exact spot that you would look. Even when you try to break up your routine, you only deviate by 15 minutes. You always choose the same newspaper stand and the same type of paper. You know it wouldn't surprise me if that older geezer keeps that brand in stock just for you. It's always untouched. That's definitely not the case with the tabloids and adult section."

Evie wasn't exactly sure what to say so she just nodded her head. A slow and unhurried movement that seemed to infuriate Ian.

Ian rolled his shoulders, clearly frustrated that Evie hadn't given him the reaction that he had expected. He growled, "Final round. All or nothing."

"Deal."

Chapter 39

The lights around the city appeared to flicker as if fearful of the pure evil that had decided to come out and play. Stars barely visible to the eye bore silent witness as their shine remained dulled behind the clouds.

"Final question. Why did I become a murderer?"

A subtle breeze blew Evie's dark hair away from her face and exposed her to Ian's cunning glare. They both knew that this was it. The question he had so carefully designed to be impossible to answer. It didn't particularly matter what Evie answered because Ian would always just claim that she was wrong.

"The clock is ticking, Evie."

"This isn't timed."

"You have until I get bored. Then I'll just kill you."

"I didn't expect another option," Evie gave a casual shrug as she tried to recall every scrawled note and shoved paper within Ian's file.

Slowly, Ian began to take small light-hearted steps in Evie's direction. He gave an impish grin and waved the knife above his head in a similar manner to how a kid on the playground would shake out a towel. Each second that Evie spent on the roof was another second that she grew closer to death.

The fact should have scared her, but instead it stirred a deep irritation. Who would know to look for Ian if she was dead? It wasn't possible to hunt a ghost that lurked in the shadows.

Closer. Evie estimated that Ian had about two more generous steps before he finally reached her. What was the answer?

Ian skipped and took another gleeful step. The gleam in his eyes was similar to a child during the holidays. Ian was close enough that Evie could see the stubble that faintly outlined his jaw. She noted how his eyes looked practically feral in the dim light.

Mere inches away.

All Evie needed to do was reach out and she would be able to touch Ian. She'd feel his furiously pounding heart as he delighted in the prospect of her demise.

Without a second to spare, Evie locked her gaze with Ian. It was a shot in the dark, but she guessed, "Because it's what you were always going to do. You always knew that it was going to happen. The where and the when were always just details leading up to it. You always fed from pain. It was inevitable."

Ian halted his advance. His body grew rigid from shock. The blade hovered a few inches above his head. He opened and closed his mouth.

One second. Two seconds. A full minute lapsed without a single word.

"You're right. Evie, you can leave, but just know that I'll be watching you."

Evie instinctively took a step back so that she could place some distance between herself and Ian. Her back hit the railing and she realized just how close she had been to winning before Ian had approached. However, the game seemed to have gone into overtime.

"I'll get going."

Evie brushed along the railing that prevented her from toppling down to unforgiving concrete below. She had no intention of falling over so close to her escape.

The shift in Ian's demeanor remained nearly imperceptible as he snickered, "I'll just have to think of you when I have my fun. I'll find a woman that looks just like you. Probably sooner rather than later. You've riled me up."

Without thinking, Evie pulled out the gun and fired.

Chapter 40

The once furious wind became a nearly inaudible whisper as blood pounded in Evie's ears. She could barely hear a thing over the sound of her own frantic heartbeat. However, she was certain that she would have heard the sound of a gunshot. Evie knew from years spent practicing on the range with Uncle Jack that a gun always gave a bit of a kick after it fired.

Nothing.

Instead, the wind continued to blow as an impish smile crept along Ian's features. The pleased look on his face told Evie everything that she needed to know.

"You gave Mrs. Haversham a jammed gun."

"It seems you're always just a second late to the party, Evie. I have to admit that I'm glad you tried to shoot me. That knowledge will make this next part so much more fun. I knew that you had a dark edge to you. We're like different sides of the same coin. You're the missing piece to my wonderful puzzle. We are both so different and yet still so alike."

Ian encroached on Evie's space as he gave his crazed comparison speech. He towered over her as the knife remained casually lowered at his side. A sick feeling settled in the pit of Evie's belly once she realized that this was finally the moment that Ian had so impatiently been waiting for. The bastard had anticipated her every move. Worse, he had nefariously infiltrated Evie's life. Even small details about her daily routine no longer felt like a coincidence. Was everything that had happened to her during the past few weeks meticulously orchestrated by this psychopath? Was everything fake?

"Do you want to know what the best part of all of this is for me?"

Ian sounded nearly thrilled as he rocked on the balls of his heels. He stood so close to Evie that she could feel the warmth of his breath against her cheek. The backs of her thighs ground against the guardrail which prevented her from plummeting to the concrete below. Evie didn't dare to take her eyes away from Ian. She kept her gaze focussed on everything, but his soulless stare. She was sure that even if she did look, his eyes would appear like endless black holes. A starless night positioned both above and below.

Endless.

Evie was stuck in purgatory.

The faintest trace of liquor mingled with Ian's scent as he waited for Evie to reply. He was looking for one final round. One last game.

Evie decided that they both were about to play one last time. The decision happened so quickly that Evie hadn't even contemplated it. The answer in her gut was second nature like flicking on a light switch when entering a dark room.

She steadied her breathing and answered what she knew to be true. Her tone was calm and her words were unhurried.

Evie knew that there was enough time to enjoy her last game.

"You like the idea that I will be the most interesting woman that you've killed. You think that toying with my life was even more fun than getting the news that your brother died in jail. Am I getting close?"

Evie tilted her head to the side and subtly inched closer to Ian. She wanted him to believe her.

The duo were so near that Evie could see a faint scar just above Ian's eye. She faintly wondered if one of his victims had managed to mark his face. A permanent warning.

It all happened so fast. One second there were two people standing on the top of Coit Tower. Bodies pressed so closely together that anyone looking at them from a distance would have assumed that they were lovers. Two people that had snuck up the stairs to steal nothing but a few innocent kisses.

In the blink of an eye, Evie kicked Ian's ankle and threw him off-balance. She gripped the top of Ian's shirt and yanked him down by his hair. Evie wrapped her arms around Ian's neck and led both of them over the side of the tower. The darkness crept in from all sides as the wind returned with a vengeance.

Somewhere in the city, a light in one of the cozy townhomes went out. It was time for slumber.

Sunday
November 3, 2019
Afternoon

Chapter 41

The crisp pages of the *San Francisco Avid Reporter* crinkled under the force exerted by slim fingers as they swiftly turned to the next page. Wild eyes flitted across the page once, twice, and then three times. He was too worked up to focus on each word so it somehow took him three passes to finally grasp all of the details. The news article was relatively small and insignificant in size. The story totaled just over a page and a half. About the size of some obituary posts.

He absently rubbed his fingers across his denim-clad thighs in an effort to wipe away the grime from the printer ink. It did little to eradicate the black substance that seemed permanently tattooed onto his skin.

Arthur leaned back in his wooden chair and took in the lush green trees that dotted the mountains. The Yosemite Valley was particularly breathtaking this time of year. A small spattering of dew danced over the blades of grass as Sequoias towered over the forest floor and reached up into the sky as if to touch the clouds.

A deep inhale caused Arthur's lungs to burn partly from the cold, but mostly from the shock of such clean thin air. It was a welcomed change from his prison cell. He had always known in his chest that Ian had set him up. Of course, there was no way that Arthur could have proved such a theory while stuck behind three feet of concrete and lodged behind unforgiving metal bars.

One thing about spending time in the slammer is that it gives you time to think. For better or for worse. Some nights Arthur had heard the sounds of grown men wailing throughout the night. Perhaps the guttural sounds were caused by getting attacked by a cell mate or finally losing it after spending so much time cooped-up alone.

Arthur thought that the most agonized groans that sometimes drifted into his cell were caused by men haunted by time. Hunted by the promise of a future that no longer existed. Plagued by a past that managed to catch up to them every single night when they were alone.

It was an endless structured cycle that Arthur grew to depend upon and simultaneously despise. Luckily, the structure and dependability of the guards allowed Arthur the ability to hatch the perfect escape plan. He had managed to bribe a guard as well as one of the prison doctors to pass him off as dead. It hadn't been a difficult task given that it was common for newcomers to try and expedite their shuffle off the mortal coil.

Arthur had thought that someone would look into his faked death, but luckily it had been quiet. He had escaped.

In all of his life, Arthur had never been happier about secretly buying a cabin in the mountains. It was relatively untraceable. A fact that had motivated him to buy it in the first place. It was a place where he was safe from his brother. Not that it seemed like his twin was going to give him anymore trouble. For all intents and purposes, Arthur was dead.

For years, Arthur had felt the weight of his twin tied around his neck. It was an inescapable understanding, Ian was eventually going to come back into the picture and kill him.

From a young age, Ian hadn't been right. It had started out slowly. Inch by inch, Ian had grown and settled into something too sophisticated to be called an outright monster and too feral to qualify as human. Ian's shadowy existence had always plagued Arthur.

After so many years spent looking over his shoulder, freedom had finally arrived. Best of all, Arthur hadn't needed to do any of the dirty work. He felt nearly giddy as he tried to steady his heart rate. It felt as if he had just won the lottery. A strange twisted sense of cosmic justice electrified his nerves. The celebration was tinged by the death of an innocent detective.

The details in the newspaper were vague, but it described a man that perfectly fit Arthur's own description. One key difference being the scar that Ian had received after a particularly rough brawl in college. At least, that's what Ian had told Arthur when he had barreled into their parent's house more than a decade ago. Now, Arthur even had his doubts about that explanation.

Arthur was willing to bet that his twin had ended up tangling with the wrong woman. Although slight and frequently bundled in tattered layers, Arthur had recognized an odd power around Evie Laythorne. She had a darkness about her. It had sent a shiver down Arthur's spine the first time that their eyes had met. He had sworn up and down that he was innocent, but Evie had never waivered. Instead she had simply dug deeper and found even more damning evidence. Evidence that in any other situation would have proved that Arthur was guilty beyond a shadow of a doubt.

In some ways, Arthur was guilty. He had known what his brother was doing and had instead chosen to stay silent. Arthur had feared Ian more than he had feared the idea of jail. He wondered if Karma would ever catch up to him for such an active omission.

Apparently, Arthur's twin had ended up at the top of Coit Tower during the early hours of the morning. Arthur was sure that the private detective had put his brother down. It's not like he blamed her. In fact, he felt obligated to one day visit her grave and thank her. She had given him the perfect opportunity to kill his old life and become reborn. On second thought, maybe a visit to her grave would be a step too far. He was no longer Arthur, after all. The perfect opportunity for freedom had changed those details.

Birds flitted through the sky as the sun unhurriedly rose above the towering trees. It was a new day.

Three people had left the city of San Francisco, but it appeared that only one had the option to return. Not that it mattered.

He didn't have a care in the world as he leisurely blew over the scalding surface of his black coffee. Steam rose from the cup like small insignificant spirits, doomed to disappear with time.

Fin.

About the Author:

Camille Cabrera is an American author and media entrepreneur. She most recently wrote THE MYSTERY OF MISTLETOE MOTEL and garnered generous media attention. Her books often center around a specific holiday and vary widely within the genres of mystery and suspense. She likes to keep readers guessing and frequently combines historical events with fiction in order to create more believable stories that balance on the realistic.

More books by Camille Cabrera:

Catalina's Tide

The Mystery of Mistletoe Motel

The Rule of Three

Coming Soon By Camille Cabrera:

Below The Water